The Inheritance

A novel

by

Gila Green

AOS Publishing, 2024
Copyright © 2024

Gila Green

ISBN: 978-1-990496-82-0

Cover Design: Jessica James

Visit AOS Publishing's website:
www.aospublishing.com

Goodbye, he says to the street signs

Goodbye, he says to a name he never liked

They will smell his name when the wind blows.

It will make sense.

Susie Berg, The Remains

*This novel is dedicated to all of those who survived their youth
living double lives.*

Chapter 1

Layne Fortunefield meticulously counted each step as she ascended the stairs to the second floor, then started over. The college exit was three flights up from her classroom, situated below street level. If she didn't make any counting mistakes, she wouldn't lose her job—this was her mantra. Some days, she occupied herself by tallying various objects like tiles, pencils, toothpicks and, of course, seconds. It helped her maintain focus.

As Layne let the heavy college door close behind her, the trek down Yonge Street, adorned with its parade of neon lights, suddenly felt interminable. Only at the street's end would she permit herself to hail an Uber. After enduring a slimeball boss like Parc day in and day out, why shouldn't she Uber everywhere? Forget saving money and forget the bus. Too many bus drivers take blind corners.

Layne's thin wool scarf clung snugly to her neck, offering a sense of protection. She adjusted it, wrapping it a bit tighter, and delved her fingers deeper into the pockets of her coat, ignoring the insistent pull of her phone. She knew if she didn't call Parc, he would undoubtedly call her. It was a matter of time. She could already anticipate the impending scenario. In her mind's eye, she envisioned Parc hesitating over his screen, ultimately choosing to phone her; texts were too impersonal for her boss.

A sense of unease settled over Layne, a feeling she labeled "iPhone separation." In her lectures, she often emphasized how our brains crave dopamine hits, readily provided by our phones. Texting, scrolling, and messaging all register as positive social stimuli, triggering a release of dopamine every time. She read that on the back of a brochure in her therapist's waiting room. In bold orange letters, the headline posed a provocative question: "Is your iPhone genuinely worth your time?"

Now, distracted by thoughts of today's workplace incident, Layne's unease intensified, centering around Parc and his intrusive actions—his whirlwind hands from her shoulder to her elbow to her palm.

As expected, the ringtone pierced the air. Layne made a deliberate choice to let her phone ring. She knew she wasn't prepared for the conversation, and she had no intention of being ready. Ring, ring—the vibrations traveled through her shoulder bag and seemed to resonate in her spine. Tension gripped her as memories flashed back, recalling the unsettling times when Parc's presence invaded her personal space, his groin brushing against her in the elevator.

Layne's resistance waned by the sixth ring. She paused on the sidewalk, fumbled through her shoulder bag, and located her phone. With trepidation, she glanced at her screen—it was him. Numbers swirled in her head 21,0,58,79,101. She took a moment to collect herself.

"Where are you?" Parc's voice broke the silence.

"On my way home," Layne said, as if Parc was unaware of her teaching schedule, prominently displayed right in front of him, along with those of seven other teachers. She allowed him to dance around the true purpose of his call, not giving him the satisfaction of addressing it directly.

Parc's voice was peppered with regret, which told her he knew her students had bailed on her today, so many that the class would have to close, but he hadn't given up and still had a life raft for her. Layne remained silent, even as he rambled on about the buckets of snow expected to fall, as though she had the slightest interest in the weather forecast.

Layne had prepaid the Uber, so when the driver pulled up to her building, she slipped out, and soon began her second ascent of the day with Parc still yapping and eating in her ear. She counted the last steps to her apartment out loud—22,23—and finally reached her front door. The blaring music emanating from inside stopped her from entering the code.

After losing her key twice, she struck a deal with Marco Monopolis, a diligent student who noticed her phone dependency and occasionally offered her headache tablets. In exchange for a dozen free English-tutoring sessions, Marco promised to install a code-lock, freeing her from the burden of keys. The code-lock served as a reminder that Marco was one of the students who had abandoned her class on the break today, disrupting the carefully constructed pieces of her life.

Layne was caught off guard by the sudden withdrawal. She had foolishly mistaken Marco's admiration and their tutoring sessions for friendship, but that was absurd when she held the balance of power. It had taken Marco stealing away from her class when she wasn't looking for the veil to lift: in her isolated existence in Toronto, she had blurred friend with friendly.

"I can't help you if you don't talk to me," Parc said. "How many?"

Not for the first time, Layne wished her boss would confine his phone calls to actual conversation, and only resort to them when a text message wouldn't suffice. He could take his food and smoke breaks on his own time.

"Fourteen," Layne answered, raising her voice to be heard over the blaring music. The attendance number on the school platform was twelve, but Parc would assume she was behind. It is a rare teacher who updates her attendance immediately after a full day of classes.

"You sure?" Parc asked, skepticism lacing his tone.

Layne's mind drifted to the jar of chocolate-covered bees that had mysteriously appeared on her desk while she was taking a break. Alongside it was a handwritten thank-you note, in what she called Spanglish, a blend of Spanish and English. The note detailed the convenience of learning online, and emphasized that it had nothing to do with Layne's "amazing" teaching.

She swallowed hard, feeling the weight of needing Parc's assistance. She cradled her phone against her neck and cracked her knuckles, the satisfying snaps providing a temporary release. It had been five years since she left home, yet she still found herself compulsively resorting to lies. It was time for the truth, Layne.

"I mean, twelve," she corrected herself.

"Both levels?" he asked.

"Thirteen in intermediate," Layne clarified.

A loose stone caught Layne's attention and she impulsively kicked it. She watched as it tumbled down the stairs of her building, gradually losing momentum until it came to a halt. She realized she hadn't given it enough force to continue its descent. As Layne listened to Parc's breathing on the other end of the line, it reminded her of a panting dog—a sound that was unbearable.

Chapter 2

"I'll have to refund their money," Parc said. "All that tuition, minus the deposit." The frustration was evident in his voice.

"That doesn't sound good."

"It's not," he admitted.

Layne taught English to foreign nursing students who needed basic language skills to pass their nursing degrees in Canada. She was happy to supply them with as many medical texts and related vocabulary as she could find online.

But there was a shift in the air this semester. Each week when Layne popped into her EFL classroom, there were fewer students to teach. Sometimes she had so many ideas flying around her brain that she was forced to pretend a headache, so she could slip outside and settle the swirl in her mind for a minute. Fewer students meant this happened more often.

"Well, it's the end of the second week. We still have another trial week to go," Parc said. "Sixty percent chose to learn online last term. It saves them—"

"Thirty-three percent in tuition fees," Layne interrupted, finishing his sentence. She quickly covered her mouth, realizing her impatience had gotten the best of her.

"And more if you include transportation and travel time," Parc added.

Layne's mouth filled with saliva and her jaw tightened. She felt her job slipping away. Soon she would be unemployed, twenty-five with an education degree, an unfinished master's thesis on child anxiety in the classroom, and a boyfriend in Johannesburg on the other side of the world. He was banned from entering Canada because the clerk at the embassy in Pretoria disbelieved Rael Hasbromman's application.

Whoever was in charge of granting visas didn't buy that Rael was interested in a third tour of Canada in as many years. They thought he was sneaking into the country to marry his fabricated girlfriend and thereby gain Canadian citizenship, so the two of them were separated until they could dream up a solution. Losing her income was a step in the wrong direction for solving her long-distance relationship.

Layne closed her eyes and tried to focus on Parc's words. She let him toss more statistics at her while he swallowed whatever aphrodisiac he was crunching on now. I'm not sure I should be talking to him when I'm this angry, she thought. It turns him on. Thinking of Rael should help.

But instead of soothing her, thoughts of her boyfriend recalled their last phone conversation. He recounted for her how a stranger on the other side of the world separated them with a stamp and a pen: "You were there for six months last year; what do you mean you're only going for travel? Tell me about your girlfriend instead, or should I say paid fiancée? Planning an illegal wedding, eh? You wouldn't be the first South African to fork over a few thousand to marry a Canadian for a passport." All of this Rael recited in a fake Canadian accent.

Whatever Rael's response to the Canadian clerk in Pretoria was, it was promptly rejected. In that instant, her dream boyfriend—the one she had met on a routine walk past Ottawa's Parliament Hill at the end of her second year of journalism school—was separated from her by entire oceans.

"Ting-a-ling. If you're daydreaming, I hope it's about me and the beach, Layney?" Parc said, infantilizing her name, which made her grip her phone harder.

She could have mouthed his words before he spoke them. In Parc's mind, the two of them lived on the beach.

"I never dream about you," she said. "I've told you nicknames are off limits and, outside of work, Parc, so are you."

"Great pity. Can't a guy dream? Layney suits you, but you know what's even better? Park Lane."

Layne put an extra layer of cold into her voice. "First, the spelling is all wrong. Second, you're British. In the U.S., it's Park Place, no connection to Lane or to me. Give it up, Parc."

Layne was unsure what was more disturbing: Parc dreaming about her, or trying to meld their names together in a board game. She would have reported Parc long ago if she had the option. There was no human resources department to report to about Parc's endless come-ons. Parc was the human resources department, leaving himself purposefully unchecked.

"Let's wrap up. If you're calling to give me notice that Rinata's got the class if you must combine them, I know," Layne said. Rinata had five years on Layne's two.

"I'm not the director," Parc said. His voice sounded counterfeit hurt. She had changed the subject back to business.

"The director wields the sword, I know that too," Layne answered.

He was lying. Parc could fire her as easily as he hired her. He was powerful when it suited him and at the mercy of his boss when it didn't. Parc had told her the same thing during her first week on the job when he asked her out for dinner after work and she rejected him, launching into a long explanation about her overseas romance.

It was a hot day in July and the sun stung their faces through the glass windows. The office was full of painters sanding down the walls, so it was impossible to focus with the scraping sounds and the fumes, increasing Layne's discomfort.

"Where in the world would a girl from Ottawa find a guy from Johannesburg? Snag an invitation to an embassy on Commonwealth Day? And that accent. Parc emphasized his own London accent. Have you actually heard South Africans speak the English language?"

"It's like a cheese grater on your ears, syllables coming and going or swallowed altogether. Oh, come on, Layney. One dinner and I'll change your mind. I can wait until you come around."

Layne bristled when Parc called her a girl, something she was sensitive to at five feet, and shut out the rest of it. After her anger dissolved, she laughed. With all of her work trying not to lie, the truth was disbelieved. Parc wasn't blind. He could see the photos of her and Rael on her WhatsApp—she managed to fit four into that tiny circle—and in her very occasional Instagram post. It was a virtual reality, if not a geographical one: Rael and Layne were a couple and geography did not matter.

Layne learned to sanitize her conversations with Parc, and to keep herself as far away from his wandering hands as socially acceptable. Given that he chose her classes and hours, she could not exactly pull a duck and fade. This was the first school she found in Toronto willing to take someone with no teaching experience and she had bills. She would handle Parc. She was so close to the finish line. She could taste her new life with Rael around the corner.

"Nice of you to call, Parc. Can't miss the bus. Peak Friday traffic out here and I need to grab a nap before the weekend hits."

If Layne had asked herself why she was lying about her location, she wouldn't have had an answer. Plus, she had zero weekend plans. She needed a therapy session to deal with the impending loss of her job, not a nap. She wouldn't get either. Her therapist was out of town this week, maybe for the month.

Layne lied compulsively, the habit was automatic, like counting. Smooth lies beat the scratchy truth. That was something fed to her like breakfast cereal from the time she could remember.

"No Uber?" Parc asked.

"Have to save my loonies, even if only loons bus in this weather. The Common Loon's off to Mexico by now." Put the brakes on the homonyms, Layne. Class was over.

"Well, everybody needs a sexy siesta once in a while," he said. "And those loons are expert hunters, too. Deep divers."

"You mean fishers?"

"As deep as they come."

"God, Parc."

"I'm trying to warm you up while you're in that winter chill, Layney. I get that you want to save your coins. Don't want to keep you."

Layne clicked off.

Don't want to keep you. Don't want to keep you. Don't want to keep you. There was a scrambled feeling in her stomach. She fought it. Parc would find her three more months of work, enough time for her to land another job. Even if it was answering phones, she would make the money she needed to start a new life with Rael. It would cost Parc more to start fresh with another teacher, and she was a natural with the students—perhaps because she had felt like an outsider all her life.

Rael: On the bus after work, my love? Good week?

Layne read with a floating-in-the-clouds smile on her lips. Any thought of Parc dissolved. Rael with his pale blue eyes and strong chest from years of high school rugby. Rael, whose hands wiped away all of her pain as soon as they met her skin. Skin-on-skin therapy. She leaned on the wall next to the front door and reread his message.

Before she could answer, another beep emanated from her phone. Jesus Christ. She longed to remain where she was, engaged with Rael online. Instead, she found herself trapped in her own personal telephone traffic jam after a full day of work that could very well be her last.

Chapter 3

Layne froze. She reread the text twice, a third time with her hand over her mouth. She only had one brother, Marvyn, and she hadn't spoken to him in five years, and sparingly before that. When he wasn't the bully of her childhood, he was the silent body in a guarded room. She could still smell his stale breath, the aroma of penicillin in what seemed to her like a dungeon, but what her mother called a juvenile holding area. Only her grandmother called it what it really was: a prison cell.

Layne's grandmother passed away when she was fifteen, and the news of her last wishes enraged her parents. In her will, her grandmother had bequeathed the house to Marvyn and Layne, but they were to claim it only when they turned twenty-one. Layne, however, was hesitant to do so while her parents were still alive- that was an understatement. Layne wouldn't dare consider it.

The will exacerbated the strain in Layne's relationship with her parents, especially at an age when she depended on them. Unfortunately, her parents were too entangled with their addiction to money and overspending to let their daughter cash in on any property. As a result, Layne chose to pretend the inheritance did not exist, steadfastly refusing to discuss it. This legacy became something she tucked away deep inside herself and buried.

Layne wouldn't so much as hear about what the value of her grandmother's property might be, and she burned all of the legal correspondence she managed to catch in the mailbox before her mother got to it. As a teenager, twenty-one was a lifetime away, and Layne finished high school as if the inheritance didn't exist.

She never brought it up with her brother and didn't want his take on it. Somehow, as usual, Marvyn ended up on the right side of her parents, even if that was the wrong side for the rest of the sane world. He was not blamed for his part in her grandmother's last wishes. But Layne wasn't underage anymore. Her family must be getting impatient for her to sell the property already. She should have made the connection by now and expected some kind of communication from them.

Still, it didn't make sense. Nothing had changed. Her answer remained: she would deal with her grandmother's gift when she was ready. In other words when her parents were either no longer alive, or mentally incapable of scheming against her to take the money away. She knew she could sign those papers from any city, any country whenever it suited her.

While Layne grappled with the unresolved issues surrounding her grandmother's inheritance, her phone beeped again. The unexpected message brought with it a new urgency.

613-375-2037: Need an answer now! He's starving!

This wasn't the first time Layne had heard of her starved brother. In prison, Marvyn's hunger strike persisted longer than the staff could tolerate, prompting a change in his location. Layne made regular hospital visits at first—weekly, then monthly—until her brother finally requested that she cease coming to the ninth floor of a small institution that, in her opinion, wasn't far enough away from their house. Though he didn't utter a word, his eyes pleaded with her to turn around and leave as swiftly as she had come.

When Marvyn finally came home, unable to make it up the stairs without a break, it did not take long for her pity to dissolve as each pound returned. If the trial and hospital had changed him, it was temporary. When Layne thought of it, images of her former self and her brother's past self in the same room hyper-focused in her mind's eye, as though illuminated by the largest flashlights in the world. It was all she could do not to shield her eyes.

Layne reread the messages for the fourth time. She didn't recognize the number and considered pressing 'block' instead of 'accept contact,' but her hand hovered, and then fell back into her pocket. She looked briefly away, then checked her phone again, imagining her desired outcome; for a moment she let herself enjoy believing what she wanted to happen. The whole thing was made up, a daydream. There was no text on her phone; she had been staring at a fake communication from an unwanted past.

Layne held her breath and checked her phone again. To her surprise, her wishful thinking didn't work, and the message didn't vanish as it was supposed to. It was much easier to think idealistically. A self-constructed future was less taxing on the brain. That's where she wanted to be.

Rael's voice in Layne's head, a balm to heal the pain of the text. He would say it so smoothly, like a cold-lipped kiss, like wet velvet. *Your brothah.*

The roar from whatever new music her roommate Virginia was blasting inside their apartment hit a new high. Virginia was famous in her social circle for her all-night parties, but Layne knew of nothing scheduled for tonight.

```
Layne Fortunefield: Who is this?
```

It was a miracle she was alone in the hallway. There were two other apartments on this floor and it was usually bustling with people coming and going, with pugs and terriers on the ends of leashes, house cats meowing behind closed doors, and buzzing phones always in the background. A familiar high-pitched laugh reached her ears. Virginia was hosting the neighbors again—two bartenders married to two veterinary assistants. Adorable, according to Virginia.

```
Layne Fortunefield: Who is this?
```

It was as though someone else's fingers were hitting the buttons. Layne's mind left her body leaning against a hallway in a residential Toronto building. She knew it was an illusion, but it didn't stop her from inhabiting it. Her new location was in her own grave; her mother, with her faded tattooed eyebrows, clinging to her father's hairy arm. Her no-longer skinny brother muttering about how young she had been.

Finally, her family of origin, the first club she was ever a member of, with only good things to say about her. She let the love warm her through the dirt and the taste of cold soil was worth it. She swallowed and opened her mouth for more. The dead were nothing if not loved, cherished, and adored. She basked in the pink glow for a few minutes, and absorbed it like a blast of sun.

It was possible to ignore the grave for this. She should have done it years ago, but she had been too much of a coward. In time her anger lowered from boil to simmer, and she carried on. She had missed out on so much.

Then she saw it. Six dry eyes, six legs with a lightness in their step as all three turned to leave, three tall waves to the cameras with their arms. Next, the applause and cheers. The bereaved family had given a grand performance and the crowd was thrilled. *Sorry for your loss, oh you poor things.*

Each word was on high volume in Layne's head. She could not take her eyes away from her family standing straighter, taller, sucking in the pity supply. The pink glow was gone, along with everything and everyone. Alone in her narrow plot, Layne realized she had made a mistake. The pressure in her skull threatened to explode, and her face was soaked with tears. It was too late, dark and getting darker. A quarter of an hour might have passed. She was so stupid, and now she was dead and stupid.

Damn this brother and the lingering effect he still had on her. A familiar tiredness crept up from the back of her neck, spreading both upwards and downwards, causing her body to sway. Layne shook her head and recognized the heaviness that enveloped her from head to toe. It was an unwanted guest; one she refused to entertain for a second longer.

The elevator door squeaked open, and the sound of lively chatter reached her. The neighbors were home. She plastered on a smile, but they were engrossed in whatever animal one of them had jumping around in a cage and steering their excited dog. They barely acknowledged Layne with a brief nod as they hurried past her.

Layne's therapist told her she would stop dissociating when she accepted that she was safe in the present. That was what she had to work on, the way she made her students write their own fairytales or new endings to old ones. Success at work was a lot about giving other people work to do.

Safe in the present. Safe in the present. Safe in the present. She deleted the text, and one piece was already back in place, the grave farther away, safety closer. Layne did not want anything to do with Marvyn. Years ago, time she had blotted out, her parents had bankrupted themselves or bankrupted someone, probably several someones, trying to keep him out of jail. But the evidence against him was too solid—unless you knew Marvyn, who could not pull off such a scam, at least not by himself. But the judge didn't know her brother. Who could blame her?

613-375-2037: *Your parents abandoned him. They'll put him back in the hospital if you don't come now!!*

Layne's energy was too diffused to resist the new message. She was catching her breath from the dissociation, smelling the dirt of her own burial plot, one she had kept in her head often growing up. Yes, she fantasized about her own grave on a regular basis for years. Something no one but her therapist knew.

Layne Fortunefield: Last time, who is this? Where did you get my number?

Layne stopped herself from typing the words on her mind. The desire to avoid echoing her parents or her brother outweighed her frustration. What she wanted to text was this:

Layne Fortunefield: What the hell do you want? Buzz off and take your sad sense of humor somewhere else.

There was not a lot she would put past her family. She could see them having a laugh, trying to freak her out, and behind it all a plan of some kind, a scheme that wasn't good for her. Layne's parents attempted to keep contact when she first left five years ago—asking, then begging her to lend them money. They lost heart after she gave nothing back but silence.

Perhaps, they harbored some misguided belief that they could wear her down this time about selling her grandmother's house. Whatever their reasons were, she did not want anything to do with it. She threw her shoulders back. She had grown up in the last five years, built a career, and met the love of her life. Whatever they wanted from her; it was not happening. Layne shivered and stamped her feet on the floor. The sounds of her determination echoed through the empty corridor. There was no more music; street noise filled the hallway. She eyed the door that she could no longer afford to rent, unless her class numbers climbed in the next day or two. An apartment full of merry, dancing neighbors was not what she needed.

There was no response to her text, but Parc sent her a thumb's-up emoji. He wasn't fooling anyone. Her class enrollment was in the red, below the sixteen-student limit. She was out of a job, and they both knew Rinata, a far more experienced employee, would teach the combined class starting next week.

The emoji was a sign that he would find her something—tutoring the weaker students or administration.

However, no one had promised her that. So far, that had been an entire conversation with Parc in her head only.

Layne rubbed her hands together. Either the temperature had dropped, or her fingers had gone numb. The life she had this morning was erasing in sections: her job, her apartment, and now this text about her brother. She didn't list the dissociation. She wouldn't go back there. One little slip didn't mean she had regressed.

Miami; Melbourne; Milan; somewhere Rael could get a visa. Layne had tried surviving in Johannesburg, but didn't last long with 'not allowed to work or freelance' stamped on a full page of her passport, once the clerk interviewing her found out her first degree was in journalism. Or the first stages of it.

The clerk waved Layne off when she said she had quit halfway, switched to education and its accompanying anxieties. He grabbed a giant stamp and put her on mute. Soon their money ran out, and she had found herself on a plane back to Canada with red puffy eyes, and enough dried tropical fruit to last her half a year.

613-375-2037: *Layne, stop pretending you don't care. He really needs you*

This time Rael was online, too. His texts were full of hearts and kisses. It was as if he shared the pit in her stomach, though that was impossible. He wasn't the type to acknowledge pits. Rael marked time with her; that's how connected they were. His breath was on her neck, his hand, tanned from the sun, on her own. She could smell his Johannesburg-scent lingering there, reminiscent of the hot sun shining down on lychee, guava, and passion fruit.

After leaving her body, pretending was her second-best talent. It was amazing how far she could go in her own mind. It worked.

The pain in her upper back released. Someone was typing again. A faceless, soundless force tapped into her phone; one determined to push her back to a place she had escaped.

Layne's heart skipped a beat. She didn't know who it was behind these words reaching out to her from nowhere. She waited. She could not dismiss them; the pull was too great. The typing stopped. Layne read because reading these texts was an irresistible compulsion for her, even stronger than her iPhone. She wanted answers about what was behind these texts, and she did not want another word.

613-375-2037: *Your parents disappeared. Two weeks ago. I was away. Neighbor found Marvyn half-starved under the table. He won't eat. If you don't come, she's turning him over to provincial custody. Old Russian witch. Do you want him to go through that again? She won't even let me in the door. Jesus Christ, you're his sister. It's me. Charlie. They won't take him away on the weekend. You're booked on the first morning flight this Monday.*

Chapter 4

Layne forwarded the texts to Rael with a short explanation. She put her phone on airplane mode and slipped it deep into her coat pocket. She had reached her limit with information; her ears bloated with it. *Russian witch?* Her brain roadblocked at: *it's me,* skimmed over to: *provincial custody,* and finally to: *Charlie.*

Marvyn had so many girlfriends over the years that Layne could not keep track. They were all more or less the same, with no family except a father in jail; no job; no education; and no ambition. Layne could only speculate that certain women were attracted to his baby-face and curly hair, making him appear far more helpless than he really was—and more innocent.

The women Marvyn dated wore too much makeup, and looked like they chronically forgot to eat. Blondes, brunettes; Marvyn wasn't picky as long as they were skinny. Charlie must have hung on longer than most. Marvyn's relationships disintegrated when one of them pegged the other as ripping them off: money; food; jewelry; cars; it didn't matter.

Layne assessed the message. She was supposed to believe her parents had disappeared. Despite her mother being sixty-one and her father sixty, they were both adept at passing for fifty, their days of successfully posing as much younger were long over. People do not vanish, and no one is kidnapping senior citizens, she thought. They might leave the country without telling anyone. That fits. She raced back down the steps of the building for fresh winter air.

Outside, Layne caught the eye of a police officer. She considered asking him if her parents had been reported missing, if he had seen their faces plastered on some posters, or on a bulletin board somewhere. She longed to hop into the back of his car and ride off with him into the night on the pretense that this was the best way to look for them, or run away from them. She wanted both. The sound of the siren would be a release. The police officer must have a car nearby. Layne pressed her elbows tightly against her sides, trying get a grip. She was already thinking crazy at the thought of flying toward her family.

A whirlwind of unsettling emotions stirred inside of her. This was a pale flicker of what happened to her when she was around them in real time, in real life. Within a mere twenty-four hours, she would catch herself mimicking them, a horrible reminder of the influence they still had on her.

"Hey, Miss Fortunefield."

Layne was caught off guard. There was no time to pull herself together. She needed grace to get through an encounter with another human being without her hysteria seeping through.

"Marco, hi. You're training to be a nurse, working as a locksmith, and delivering pizza, too?"

Her voice ended on a high pitch, anger stirring in her stomach as she recalled the events of the morning. Marco did not even have the courage to tell her he was dropping out of her class to her face, sneaking out instead on the break, and now here he was. She planted her heels into the pavement, trying to get the world to carry her.

"Yeah. Multi-tasking, you know? New door code working out? Must be nice not having to worry about your keys anymore," Marco said.

"One worry goes and one comes," Layne answered.

Marco nodded, gesturing toward the pizza with his chin. "I do this part-time, you know, until I pass English and can work as a nurse. The locksmith thing, I picked up from my dad—not official."

Layne could not help but marvel at Marco's articulate spoken English, yet it remained a puzzle how he struggled with reading and writing. He wasn't the first student she had encountered with this unique blend of language skills, adept at absorbing conversational English from movies and television, but keeping clear of books. Unfortunately for these students, oral language wasn't enough; the path to becoming a nurse in Canada demanded a level of proficiency in both reading and writing.

Layne checked the address on the bill. "Let me help you. You need to go two buildings down, about 200 steps away." She jerked her head in the right direction. The silence between them lingered longer than it should have. Marco broke it.

"I'm sorry about today. "

Layne held up her hand to quiet her former student. It was better he didn't uncover any emotions. It was risky for Layne to display her feelings about what it meant to her to lose her job. She hadn't seen Rael in months. Now, with this text about her brother on top of it, this was not a good time. They both knew what happened.

First, Marco waited for her to go to the bathroom, then he left that note on her desk. Reviewing it in her mind only pushed her closer to the edge. She had a thing about deceit. He should have been straight with her, given her a chance to tell him that she would lose her job if attendance dropped.

"Sneaking out on the break was stupid."

"I understand," Layne said. She rocked on her toes. This was her biggest lie today. She didn't understand at all. They should have allowed her to explain that their chances of passing the course were higher staying in the class, and it was only a matter of time before it goes hybrid, with at least two days a week at home.

"King and Angel wanted your opinion, but I'm in a money cruncher."

"What did we say about slang in class?"

"You don't have to teach me anymore."

Layne could not stop herself. It had all been too much. She stepped closer to Marco. Too close.

"You want to know what I understand?" she said. Her generosity had run dry. "That I spent hours of my own time—no, weeks, way beyond what we'd agreed in exchange for the lock—

helping you pass your entrance exams, and you could not be bothered to tell me you were quitting the class and taking your buddies with you. You didn't give a second thought to what it would mean for me."

Layne's fists clenched, and she was in her former student's face. She watched in slow-motion horror as Marco hopped back, missing the curb, and a split second later, his pizza crashed onto the pavement.

"What the hell was that?" he yelled, his voice filled with frustration. He swiftly pulled out his phone and began capturing the scene. "You think I'm some kind of idiot?"

"It was an accident." Layne struggled to regain her composure. She slid on an icy patch, falling on top of Marco. "What's with the camera?" She scrambled to stand. "What are you doing? Hey, stop with the video."

"Like hell I will. I know how to protect myself in this country. You're always asking about my jobs, like they have something to do with you. Maybe you're working for them, huh? Maybe you're the one always trying to get the foreigners fired. King and Angel suspected you, too. I should have known."

"What are you talking about?" Layne grabbed at his phone, but Marco darted out of the way. Now on his knees, soaking them, Marco hovered over the fallen pizza. The cardboard box had opened, revealing bits of dirt sticking to the cheese, whether from the pavement, or his hands, or passing cars, she could not tell.

Marco's eyes darted nervously. "I've seen a lot. You wouldn't understand. They're always watching. Always. I've got evidence now."

Layne sighed, realizing that Marco's belief in conspiracy theories colored his perception of everyday events, making even a pizza mishap a potential act of sabotage in his mind.

"It was an accident," Layne pleaded, scanning the area for the police officer, but he was long gone. "I'm so sorry."

"I've got great video, too," Marco said. There was bitterness in his voice. He gestured to the ruined meal. "See this? You wrecked the entire order." He kicked the waterlogged pizza, but it didn't budge. "Do you have any idea what this means? The customer's already telling off my boss right now, and who knows what else they're saying? It's always like this, someone out to get the outsider."

"I didn't mean to do this," Layne said. "Let me pay for it."

"I don't want anything from you." He twirled his finger in circles next to his ear. "This is just another piece of evidence for your secret agenda, right? Always watching, always plotting. Well, it won't work. You can't fool me."

Marco raised his hand in front of him as if she might attack him, and picked up the wet cardboard box, which threatened to topple again. He grabbed it with both hands and dumped it into a trash can. Then he stormed down the road. If something happened before that, if more was said, already Layne didn't remember. That feeling of separation from her body had taken over. Use the body to control the mind, her therapist said.

"Wait!" She waved her hands in the air. "Let me pay, please." It was an accident, a mistake. All she wanted him to do was understand. Layne's mouth ran dry. She had to regain control of herself. She hoped that Marco, despite his current mistrust, would eventually calm down. He had always been a nice guy, though distinguishing his paranoia from genuine anxiety, and his superstitions from conspiracies, wasn't always easy.

This was the first time his suspicions had been directed at her. Still, for Layne, he was a friend, and she didn't have many of those. The words skimmed through her mind. Other platitudes joined in: This would blow over. From lemons comes lemonade. What a load of crap.

Marco owed her nothing. She should never have come back outside. She should have gone home and stayed there. Parc would not so much as let her clean the office if he heard about this, not unless she gave him what he wanted. This is all Marvyn's fault, she thought, or her parents, or whoever set Charlie up to contact her.

Charlie's text messages were already sucking her in, pushing her to close her own doors here, so her only path would take her where she shouldn't go. It was a game whose rules were engraved into her core, and that first text was like the first roll of the dice. That was what she needed to get into her head.

By responding, even with one short text, she had jumped on the board. These games sunk her brother, who thought he would grow up to be like daddy, but ended up begging for daddy's help instead, while he lay on the floor in a cell, resentment filling the invisible holes that punctured him, like a bullet through a skull. Well, Layne won't make a move.

"Everything okay, miss?"

Layne's heart skipped a beat as her eyes met the gaze of a police officer nearby. The sudden appearance of a cop triggered an instinctive fear within her. Had he witnessed the entire scene with Marco? Panic surged through her veins. She mumbled a response, thrust her hands deep into her pockets, and quickened her pace, careful not to break out into a run.

When she was sure the cop was long gone, she rested against the side of a building and tried to get her bearings. Dark clouds gathered overhead in the cold sky. The phone got Layne's attention again. She turned up the ringer. Rael had sent half a dozen messages and phoned as many times, but she didn't want to share more, and she wasn't ready for his sunshine take on things.

Layne could recite what Rael would say if she hinted her job was over: "Nothing lasts forever. It was a job teaching English; the world was full of them: as common as dirty dishes. Whatever you're worried about no longer exists. You're not a weak girl anymore. You're a strong, sexy woman in charge of your own life. I'll be available by phone 24/7, and we'll deal with it. I'm with you all the way."

Or worse. "This was perfect. Just when you didn't have a place to stay and lost your job, you got called home. How's that for luck?"

Rael had no idea how contagious home was, how the grotesquely familiar took over and sucked you between its long fangs, remade you in its own image like God under the brand-new sun, busy with Adam's rib.

Still thrown by the incident with Marco, Layne searched for her parents' numbers on her phone. She would tell them what she thought of this latest prank. The numbers weren't listed under anything as normal as "mom and dad" or "parents." Layne used exclamation mark emojis instead.

One for her mother, two for her father, and a tornado emoji for Marvyn because he burned everything he touched, or it burned him first. One way or the other, it disintegrated. The phone rang somewhere in space. She tapped her foot, waiting to explode at the first hello. Nothing. Her brother's number led to the same result. The last call was to the Toronto airport.

It took her ten minutes to confirm that she had a ticket to Ottawa. If she had looked properly at her text messages, she would have seen the airline confirmation. There were so many spam advertisements these days, her eyes had glazed over it. It was snowing now as Parc had warned her. He was like Layne's personal prophet sometimes, his words full of predictions and admonishments.

Buckets of hard, white snow blurred her vision and made their way down the back of her neck. Handfuls of the frozen flakes were trapped in Layne's curly hair, pressing the cold deeper into her skin. This time, she bolted up the stairs to her apartment without counting.

Chapter 5

As Layne reached her door there was only silence, but the neighbor's phone was ringing off the hook. It had one of those fire alarm ringtones deliberately picked to drive anyone who heard it crazy. The jarring sound echoed through the hallway, disrupting her attempt at tranquility. With both hands over her ears, Layne punched in the code Marco had inserted for her, and let herself in. Inside, it was impossible to tell that anyone had been there, let alone a gathering. Everything was spotless.

"Virginia?" Layne called. She wiped her wet boots on the mat. "I'm home."

The place smelled of the new leather couch Virginia bought last week at the request of her boyfriend James, who was "into leather everything," according to her. The odor fused with that of the wet clothing Virginia insisted on hanging all over her bedroom, that would take days to dry in winter. She wouldn't consider machine washing her silk lingerie and scarves, and a dryer was out of the question. No doubt James liked silk with his leather.

James was Parc's boss, the director he was always referring to, his voice unable to filter his envy.

"Wish I could afford that," Parc said when James pulled up in his Tesla, even if it was the second time that day. Not to mention his endless references to James "wielding the sword" and "opening doors" that Parc himself somehow found slammed in his face.

This connection to her roommate only made things worse for Layne, who swore she would keep a high wall between her job and the rest of her life once they were officially a couple. She wasn't allowed to utter a syllable of criticism about Parc to Virginia, and certainly not to James, who was fifteen years Virginia's senior at 40 years old, and desperate for Virginia's attention.

Layne was bursting to share her day with Virginia, but the apartment had the stillness in the air that told Layne no one was home. There was a faint cigarette smell, but nothing more. She could not understand it. There was laughter, music, and chatter when she was hunched over her phone in the hallway.

How long had she been outside with Marco? Time closed like a fist over her more often than she cared to admit. She flung off her boots and they thudded against the wall. The neighbor's phone continued to ring.

Layne swung her front door open again with a surge of frustration. "Could you answer your goddamn phone?" she screamed. Beep, beep, beep, pause, beep, beep, beep. Then the wail of a baby from another floor, a television blaring too loud. Layne slammed her door shut, locked it, and pulled a winter hat over her ears.

Frustration brewed within Layne as she yearned to zap Virginia home and escape into someone else's life for a while. Her roommate would chat in French about her day at the cosmetic counter; the forty-year-old men and women who asked her to transform them into thirty-year-olds, and the thirty-year-old men and women who asked her to wave her magic wands and make them look twenty.

The next step eluded Layne, leaving her wrestling with uncertainty. Dabbling at a keyboard in front of a screen would allow her mind to wander to places she didn't want to go. She counted to ten, then fifty, then 100. She searched for something to do with her hands, and straightened out the front closet, rehanging a couple of coats about to fall to the floor, folding the scarves, and sorting the gloves into a neat pile.

Three years ago, Virginia Saint placed an advertisement on a Facebook group for a roommate, and Layne saw it while she was riding on the Greyhound bus that brought her the 218 miles from Ottawa's downtown station to Toronto's Scarborough Town Centre. Layne clicked through the photos of low shots in natural light designed to make the place appear more spacious, as if they made any difference. The price was right and that was all that mattered.

When she left her parents, Layne dormed at Carleton University and studied journalism, but after two years, she finally had the guts to admit that journalists were bottom feeders, waiting for others to act. She had had a lifetime of that. Every second of Layne's youth had been biding her time to see what her parents would do, so she could keep one step ahead. Were they about to lose the house again? Their jobs?

Layne needed to prepare herself for whatever train wreck was coming. No way she was setting herself up for another career in people watching. So, she didn't need Carleton's prestigious journalism school after all. She could move to Toronto, cut geographical ties with her parents, and switch to education, something that made her the one to act. She had taken enough courses to make the transition without losing more than a semester of studies.

The truth was Ottawa, at only 2790 square kilometers, sitting on the Ottawa River with Parliament Hill as its center in the east of southern Ontario, wasn't big enough for all of the Fortunefields. Layne had to leave the capital, home to the most educated population of all Canadian cities, with its boats on Rideau Canal in the summer, and skaters in the winter. She needed to escape the smothered feeling that Ottawa gave her, as if she were always breathing through a tube, wads of paper lodged in her throat.

On the bus, Layne texted as fast as her fingers could type, and sent a month's rent by bank transfer during the first twelve minutes of the ride. The bus was clean and comfortable, but there were no charging points. That worked to Layne's advantage, her phone had so little charge when she boarded that she could not change her mind. Ottawa was over. Her text message was confirmed before her phone displayed low battery in a red bar across the top. That five-year-old decision turned out to be one of the best of her life, and no cryptic text message would change that.

Layne plunked her briefcase on her desk, used the bathroom, and washed her hands, face, and neck. Making herself a cup of coffee, she retreated into her bedroom. There, she grabbed her laundry basket. She piled her work clothes—seven silky choose-a-shade-of-beige blouses and five mid-calf, choose-a-shade-of-black skirts— into the washing machine. Only pajamas would be needed tomorrow. Work clothes were for people who had jobs.

The idea of logging into her class online made her hands shake. She took a deep breath and summoned the strength to type her code into the keyboard. Delete those photos, Marco, please. Sure, you were my student, but you'll graduate soon enough, and then I thought we could be friends. Anyone watching could see it was an accident. There were no recently added photos or video. Nothing. An anxiety-filled balloon popped in her mind.

Layne ignored the internal voice that asked her why she would imagine Marco would do her a favor, and why she had logged off and begun looking for her suitcase. No, never a suitcase. A carry-on. She hauled it out of the back of her closet and left it on her bed. But she was not ready to open it. She needed more to do with her hands. The dishwasher. At least Virginia had left her that to do. She unloaded the wine and vodka glasses. Virginia lived for entertaining at night, another thing that tortured her older boyfriend.

Possibility one: Layne's parents snuck out on vacation to put some space between themselves and the son who hardly left the house. Leaving the house was first on the list. Marvyn never put a bank account in his own name. Another strike against him at twenty-nine years old.

Possibility two: They both waited for him at their new address after the bank evicted them, and her brother refused to believe it.

Another option: her father convinced her mother to move back out West—he had always longed for his hometown, Vancouver—and her brother took a stand. He would show them, force them to bend to his will and stay in Ottawa. They had a fight. Her parents took off, Marvyn chose to strike: first his mind, then his body.

Layne's mind coasted along the answers to the riddle as she rinsed the glasses and dug around for the dishwashing soap. She asked herself which version spoke to her the most, the one that felt right in her body when she said it out loud. The half-starved brother under the table part she bought. She had seen him that way herself many times, a one-man demonstration.

Once at a museum in Montreal, Layne watched a protest exhibit, images of dissent all over Europe: Poland, Italy, France. She was mesmerized, observing the juxtaposition of people from disparate cultures rallying against their governments, and the reactions from the various police forces against their citizens. Marvyn could have fit into any of those angry groups, crying out as the leader of the pack.

Chapter 6

It was rare to find a home without an entrance or hallway in Toronto, but somehow Virginia had pulled it off. When the front door opened, you were instantly in the living room, right in the middle of the action or the emptiness, something Layne always found unsettling.

Layne could use a hallway right now to block off the view of her in the kitchen and give herself a moment before having to face anyone, should Virginia return. But her only other option was to eat her Greek yogurt with almond butter and sliced dates in her bedroom, which resembled more of a WW2 bunker with its low ceiling and a window that was no larger than a shoebox-sized pane of glass. There was no dining room and Virginia was strict about eating in the living room. The rumble of the dishwasher filled the kitchen. A door opened and closed. Was someone here?

"Hello," Layne called.

Silence. Layne missed Virginia. She considered having someone to talk to a luxury after a lifetime of keeping things to herself, and it was something she had gotten used to in Toronto. Virginia was the closest thing to a friend Layne had. She had adjusted to her own company over the years and didn't have much time to socialize between teaching full time, after-class tutoring, and spending any free moment online with Rael. This was not a dilemma with Virginia around. Her roommate caught every party announcement, and was the type to get free tickets to events if she was willing to post them to her thousands of followers on her social media pages.

"Are you finally ready to talk to me?" Rael asked, when Layne answered the phone on its fifth ring. An hour had passed since the collision of texts. "Digging out your suitcase?"

"Yes and no," Layne answered. The flight from Toronto to Ottawa was not much longer than a lunch break. Her empty carry-on balanced on the edge of her bed, but she had made no motion to dust it off or open it. She had put all of her clothes in the washing machine. Her next rent payment was due in ten days, and that meant dipping into her savings, which was only peddling backward, away from Rael. This wasn't the plan. Rael was the plan. The only plan.

"What is this business about your job? Your brother? Your parents?" Rael said brother like *brothah* and parents the way Layne would say *pair-ents*. "And who sent you that text?"

"I forwarded you what I know. Charlie's not worth discussing." This had some truth to it. Layne saw a few girlfriends of Marvyn's in her mind and wasn't sure which one was Charlie. Good chance she had mismatched faces to bodies. Layne found herself whispering into the phone.

"Why don't you start at the beginning?" Rael coaxed.

"There's nothing more," Layne said.

"I have all the time in the world."

"What do you mean?" Layne asked. "And I don't. I'm ready to sleep."

"Let me know when you're ready to talk, Layne. It's important, especially with your brother involved. I've been trying to reach you for more than an hour, and we've talked about getting stuck in your thoughts before. We've got a lot to cover, and I'm here to help you through it."

"What?"

"I mean open the door, doll. Hey, I'm outside."

Chapter 7

Layne raced to the door and peeked through the keyhole. The light in the corridor was broken, making it impossible for her to see anything but shadows. This threw her. It wasn't broken when she arrived. Could it have fizzled out so recently? Had someone turned it off? She had to fight to shut down her mind that leaped for explanations for any changes in her environment faster than she could keep up with them.

Disappointment weighed heavily on Layne as she searched for Rael in the gloomy hallway, even as she told herself it was crazy to do so. Virginia's absence was getting to her. Not to mention the void of her boyfriend and the painful loss of her job. She hugged herself, then squeezed, and brought her shoulders up to her neck. She counted to eight and released them, letting go of her sides. The only sound behind the door was the neighbor yelling about how someone should shut up that dog for once. Rael was only trying to make her laugh. He was big on practical jokes.

Layne felt a mix of emotions—grateful for the attempt at humor, yet frustrated. She would call him back and tell him she didn't appreciate him getting her hopes up after the day she'd had. She pressed his number on her phone, ready to give it to him, when a sudden doubt crossed her mind: was sharing a laugh exactly what she needed?

Then, a male voice hummed an African beat, hands slapping against a wall in imitation of a drum. Her heart fluttered. Her hands shook. She flung open the door.

"Got you," Rael said.

She squealed. Then she was in his arms, slapping him on the back for tricking her. Rael grabbed her hands, kissed her on both cheeks, and brushed her lips with his. He tasted like sweet chutney sauce, mango, and golden raisins.

"See how much I love you? Even when you make me wait an hour after flying for thirty-six," he said. "I can't keep my hands off you."

Layne didn't speak. She was too taken aback. Rael was here. In Canada. In her building. Eight months had passed since the last time she said goodbye to him at the Toronto Pearson International Airport, her heart breaking as she pulled away from him. What about that clerk in Pretoria? Had Rael's whole visa story been a plan to surprise her? Layne smelled something sour and made a face. The front of her blouse was wet.

"Did I mention there was a baby beside me on the plane?" Rael said. He still had his arms around her waist. "When she wasn't sleeping, she was vomiting. Mom flew by herself."

"Good thing I did so much laundry," Layne said. "But the smell." Layne waved her hand in front of her nose.

"Terrible," Rael said, holding his own nose. "Now we'll both have to shower. It's a sacrifice I'm willing to make." He mentioned a few things before that, but Layne never heard them. He took her hand and led her back inside the apartment, dragging in his suitcases, and locking the door. It was all Layne could do to keep her hands off him.

"Admit it, you were hoping I'd say that," Rael said.

"Say what?" Layne could not stop looking at Rael. Eight months was a long time, and the reality of him standing in front of her was surreal. As they entered the apartment, she marveled at the four suitcases and two handbags he brought with him. It was a lot, maybe even triple the usual amount.

"About the shower," Rael said, pulling her attention away from his luggage.

"Did you get Virginia out of the house, too?" Layne asked.

Rael wiggled his eyebrows in response, then dropped his coat, attempting to hang it up. It fell to the floor.

"I'll get it later," she said.

"Get that look off your face. Have you never been teased before? This is the best surprise ever, isn't it?"

"I should have known," she answered. "Is the 6 a.m. flight and brother story bogus? Please say yes." For a second, Layne allowed herself to feel elated, free; not the stone she turned into when it came to her brother. Her family pulled her into an emotional cave, one she was careful never to visit.

Rael held up both hands. "Why would this girlfriend make it up?"

"Anyone willing to date Marvyn is capable of anything."

"You're being ridiculous. I read the texts. You forwarded them to me, remember? The situation sounds serious."

Layne shut out the rest of her thoughts. She kept her eyes on Rael as he unzipped his short black boots, picked up his coat, and hung it in the cupboard, then slid his suitcase next to the wall by the front door. Part of her feared this was an illusion. His presence. But her room was bursting with his possessions. He was real. She marveled at how he managed to get his plants through customs, but didn't bother to ask.

Having traveled with Rael enough, Layne knew he held back in line until he spotted a free female customs officer. Then, he disarmed her with chat, his accent, his charm until his traveling business was already on the other side of the border. No doubt he would have a mini laboratory set up by tomorrow night filled with plants the Canadian government wouldn't have let over the border. He disappeared into the bathroom for five minutes–the toilet flushing, bristles on teeth, running water.

"I suppose I should have asked if you have weekend plans?" he said when he came out, drying his hands on a towel.

"Never too late," she said. "Ask me now." She made a show of flipping through her diary. She still kept a physical diary for class notes and new ideas, and a travel one in her purse.

Rael bent on one knee. "I love you, Layne. Are you free this weekend, so I can show you how much? And for the rest of your life after that?"

"Hmm," Layne said. "Weekends are tough and the rest of my life? My calendar is so full." She frowned at him. "People have no idea the number of hours teachers work after class, entire summers devoted to professional development and all those educational committees."

"Didn't you hear me say I love you?" He stood and took her hands in his.

She held his fingers and never wanted to let them go. "For the rest of your life, you say?"

"At least."

Layne raised herself onto her toes and kissed him.

Soon, he had maneuvered her onto her bed. Her heart swelled as he kissed her deeper and the warmth of his skin joined with hers. She had not realized how much she had missed him, needed him, wanted him. Rael pulled back and pushed her hair off her face and they smiled at each other.

"We have the whole weekend together before your flight," Rael said. "Unless you want me to come with you."

This suggestion hit Layne like salty caramel ice cream, sensory overload.

"Nothing on earth would make me want to introduce you to my brother or my parents, if they show up by then."

"I can see this is about you and your family, not me being here, right?" Rael crossed his arms over his chest. He reached out to take Layne's hand, but she pulled away. "What's with that look on your face?" he asked.

"I get the feeling you're not always listening when I tell you my family's toxic." Her fingers tapped against her thigh.

"But maybe, with us here together, we can figure it out. You don't have to face it alone," Rael suggested, a reassuring tone in his voice.

Lane stood and paced. Her blood boiled too easily on this subject. It was unfair of her to be upset when he had flown across the world to see her.

She picked up the items on her dresser—a Kent hairbrush, a bottle of Boardwalk Essence perfume, her favorite calming peppermint spray—and banged them back into place. Her happiness at reuniting with Rael had a bitter edge. It felt as though she was losing control.

Instead of enjoying her boyfriend's arrival, she had to leave town, and she could because her job was unofficially over with formal notice mere days away. Nothing that transpired today could she have ever imagined when she woke up this morning. The washing machine beeped.

"Go on," Rael said.

In the laundry room, Layne yanked open the washing machine door, slammed it shut in frustration, and pressed too hard on the buttons. The last thing she wanted was to sound shrill, so she didn't speak.

"By Monday morning, this neighbor's throwing your brother into provincial custody and from what you've told me, that's serious," Rael said. He had followed her. She was hoping he had fallen asleep on her bed.

"I see you're still on this subject," she answered.

Layne led Rael back to the bedroom, her arms full of clean clothes. The atmosphere had changed. She would sort her clothes and change it back.

"I still smell like baby vomit," Layne said. "What about that shower?"

"He could hurt himself there and maybe it would help if I was around."

"You trust those texts too much," Layne said.

"You don't think your brother could hurt himself?" he asked. "Or you don't think I could help you with your brother?"

"I don't think anyone can help my brother."

"Your therapist said that you're challenged by absolute thinking. Try to see things more nuanced, remember? Does it make sense that no one could help your brother? You think I don't remember because it's a Zoom session?"

"That's how you interpret him."

Rael held out his hand and Layne took it. They relaxed side by side on her bed. Her cynicism was all over her, her lack of charity toward her brother tangible, until she felt the tension return, gripping her neck and shoulders.

"You don't really believe your brother's beyond help," Rael said. He rested on his side with one hand tangled in her hair. "You made sure the phone numbers you tried were correct?"

Layne nodded. Another lie. No one had answered those numbers.

"So then?" Layne covered her eyes with her hands. "We can't be responsible for your brother getting locked away somewhere, my darling, right? And it might be a lot for you to handle."

"Might be the best place for him," Layne snapped.

"Listen to you," Rael said. He stood, eyed Layne, his hands on his hips. "He's your only sibling. Family!"

"Notice we never speak," she answered.

"Come on," he said. "You told me he got taken by his best friend to swallow the rap for some scam. He was barely out of his teens. And he needs you. You might be surprised at how nice it is to feel needed."

He pulled her up to him and whispered in her ear. "Fine. I won't accompany you if it upsets you this much. I can find my way around Toronto until you get back, but you'll owe me big time for only giving me one weekend when I've waited so long." Layne held Rael close.

"I'm willing to pay," she whispered in his ear.

Chapter 8

Layne let Rael's hug drain all of the tension from her body as she breathed into his neck and rubbed her cheek against his rough skin. An overwhelming sense of regret for all the love she had missed in the last eight months engulfed her. Rael was always right, which drove her nuts, except when he was wrong. Her inability to believe this text message made her sound heartless. Marco and his friends skipped out of class, then Rael and Virginia pulled one over on her; all in one day. Why not someone else? Her phone rang. Virginia's name flashed on the screen.

"Hello?" Layne said. "You're on speaker." Layne crawled back into Rael's arms. She stared at the white world out the window as she listened; it was snowing all this time.

"Got you," Virginia said. "It was so adorable how Rael contacted me to surprise you. Surprised?"

Then she laughed so hard there was no point in Layne answering her, and she had to pull the receiver away from her ear. Layne laughed with her.

"You're the best. Thanks for helping him out."

"You don't have to thank me. You're one lucky girl, eh? Your Rael is a catch, so romantic with that accent, and now you have him for the whole weekend. I've made other plans. Enjoy your time alone."

Layne hung up and texted Virginia an oversized thank-you emoji. She tried not to respond when Virginia called Rael a catch, so texting was easier. She told herself she should be flattered by her roommate's praise of her boyfriend, but instead she saw Virginia with her breezy smile, holding the hand of another woman's husband, someone's father. Layne spent a lot of time teaching her students that Canadians expect you to mind your own business.

"Did I hear her say romantic?" Rael said. He sat straighter and posed with one hand behind his head and one on his hip.

"Don't let it go to your head," Layne said. "She's a mega flirt. Does it for sport."

"Did I say flirt?"

"No. I did. She makes me feel cold sometimes, everybody loves Virginia."

"Hey, no sketchy vibes," Rael said. He pulled her close. "I love you enough for everybody. Now you're mine all weekend."

Rael tackled Layne and pinned her to the bed before she could respond and tickled her sides until she screamed for him to stop. He released her and got busy unloading his belongings. Already his toothbrush was next to hers, his cologne in a drawer, his wallet on her side-table.

It turned out to be a great day after all. The plane to Ottawa might be taking off on Monday morning, but Layne wouldn't be on it. It was a trap, and she wasn't interested. Rael would agree with her soon enough. She got it that it was hard for other people to understand how she needed to be unanchored from her family permanently.

The phone rang again.

"Forgot to tell you," Virginia said when Layne answered. Her tone was different this time and Layne moaned. She closed her eyes and tried to see the calming darkness behind them.

"Maybe later," Layne said. There was a hint of pleading in her voice. She so much wanted to enjoy being with Rael again, and the world was determined to take it away from her.

"I want to catch up with Rael before he falls asleep," Layne said. Another lie, another lie. Rael could not look more awake. He had already noticed a missing lightbulb and asked her with hand gestures where he could find another. She indicated the bathroom cupboard. Her favorite thing about this apartment was her private bathroom that was the same size as the bedroom.

"Wait, it's important. Someone called Mrs. Polina Voloskovich left a message. Know her?"

Layne shook her head, as though Virginia could see her. Voloskovich. Russian witch.

"Something about a brother," Virginia continued. "I didn't know you had a brother."

Virginia paused but Layne pretended not to notice that her statement was really a question. "Anyway, he's cramping her style. I told her you'll turn on your phone after work or on your break, but she said she didn't know if she would get another chance to call. Sounded urgent. My ride's here. Gotta go."

Layne hung up. Rael whistled as he cleared some space on a shelf, then the closet. He switched to humming. There were neat piles of socks, underwear, t-shirts, and bottles of creams and lotions of his own making. Rael was an aspiring herbalist, something his lawyer parents and brother looked down on, which only motivated him more.

"All right," Layne said. "Stop pretending. I know you heard that." She spoke to the floor. Rael kept working, but he wasn't humming any longer. "Mrs. Voloskovich must be the one Charlie wrote about in her text," Layne continued.

Maybe something was going on there. Nobody said anything for a minute, but the expression on Rael's face told her this was a test she had to pass. It was as if he was silently urging her to do the right thing.

"I'll go stock the fridge," Layne said finally. "Wait with him until my parents show up if Charlie can't, but not for more than a couple of days."

"It's the right thing to do." Rael sauntered over to the bathroom as though he had been living here forever, his movements broad, sweeping. She loved that about him, his comfort wherever he was, so different from her own relationship to space and how much of it she deserved. He ran the tap.

"There's only enough hot water for one," Layne said. "It's a shame to waste water."

"Is that so?" Rael pulled Layne to the bathroom and closed the door.

"I'm serious," Layne said.

"About what? No, not now. Shhh," Rael said. "You do this all the time. You settle and then you renege." He put a finger to her lips. "Prisoners aren't allowed to talk."

"Am I your prisoner?" Layne asked.

"Yes," Rael said. He slipped his warm hands under her shirt and unhooked her bra. "You're most definitely my prisoner."

Layne's stomach dropped. She needed to organize herself if she was heading out of here on Monday morning, but she yearned to give in to Rael's warm fingers, kneading her shoulders. There was soft music coming from somewhere. His phone? He so had her number.

Rael whistled a jazzy tune in her ear. The wall heater was already on, and the flower-shaped candle next to the sink gave off a rose-petal scent. He backed her up against the door and the light went off, leaving them in the glow of candlelight. She looked into his penetrating eyes and let him kiss her deeply on the mouth.

Rael pulled the turtleneck over her head, careful not to catch her shirt on her rose gold studs. The ones delivered to her last month because he missed her, plus his own homemade bottle of hand cream.

"Prisoners can only wear jewelry," he whispered into her ear. He bit her neck. Layne felt his hardness against her thigh and closed her eyes. She was not fighting anything anymore. Rael kissed her neck, her stomach down to her belly button. She saw his head moving over her body, his tongue going in and out flicking her skin. She watched him undress her, throw her clothes in a pile, down to her underwear.

He clicked the lock closed, turned on the shower, kissed her down one arm and then the other and led Layne into the steaming hot spray. He soaked her long curly hair and opened a bottle of pomegranate shampoo that he had brought with him. He emptied some into the palm of his hand, turned Layne around so her back was to him and washed her hair slowly, massaging with two hands, pressing the tops of his thighs into hers.

Layne had already forgotten her long day at work, her phone call with her boss, the low attendance hanging over her job, the shocking text message, even the disastrous meetup with Marco. There was no stress about the journey before her. Her mind was filled with her boyfriend and soon so was her mouth, her arms, her thighs, her calves. Rael soaped her entire body, slowly, the way she liked it, all the way down to her toes. Then it was her turn and she was massaging his shampoo; rubbing his strong, hard chest, his arms. All at once, Rael grabbed both of her hands together at the wrists.

"Who said you're allowed to touch me, prisoner?" he asked. He bit her neck. "Now you're in trouble."

"Oh no," Layne whispered. "I don't want trouble."

Rael backed her into a corner of the shower and raised her up by her hips. He entered her easily. She inhaled, her back was pressed into the cold tiles.

"Too late," he said into her ear.

Layne moaned and pushed as deeply into the wall as she could, enjoying the cold tiles against her hot, wet skin. She gripped Rael around the waist with both of her legs and rocked against him. When they were done, he held her in the shower, whispering in her ear how much he loved her, and it was time for them to talk about his application for permanent residency. He covered her shoulders with small kisses until the water ran cold.

Chapter 9

The living room Layne shared with Virginia was a tiny oasis with sea blue walls and an eye-catching, multi-armed, glittering chandelier arranged to look more like a fireworks display. Fueled with fresh coffee and the excitement of being alone for the whole weekend, it felt like she and Rael were traveling again—like when Rael took Layne to Table Mountain in Cape Town and there was nothing but endless ocean, the two of them on the hunt for hyraxes, porcupines, mongooses, and tortoises. Rael would have been delighted to come across a snake, too, but Layne was grateful when they didn't.

Here in her living room, finally with Rael, she could pretend they were escaping from real life. It was Saturday morning and Monday was still far away.

"I see you're dressed for Canada in February," Layne said, eyeing Rael in his black boxer shorts, with his flat stomach and broad shoulders.

Rael stared down at his boxers, as though he was surprised to find he wasn't wearing anything else. "Pleased that you like them. Matching pair for you in my case," he said. He pointed to her bedroom.

Layne got off the couch where she had been sipping her coffee and squinted her eyes, bending eye level with his waist, pretending to study the shorts. "Wow, you knew exactly what I wanted."

"Hey, let's try yours on right now. Don't bother looking through my suitcase, they're one-size. You can try mine."

Within seconds, Rael had slipped his boxers off and put them over her own cotton underwear, which was all she was wearing under her barely-tied, fleece housecoat.

"Perfect," he said, before he slipped off both pairs of underwear, and eased her onto the couch. With his naked body on top of hers, Layne closed her eyes and concentrated on the warmth of his skin. Rael tangled his hands in her hair at the back of her neck and wound his fingers in her long curls.

"Mmm," he whispered in her ear. "Your hair smells so good. It's the inspiration for my new conditioner line. I need to learn how to bottle this scent of yours."

"When you're a famous brand, will I be on the bottle?" She propped herself on one elbow, pushing her back into the side of the couch.

"Front and back," Rael said. He caressed her hair as he kissed her and stuck the fingers of his other hand in both of their mouths before reaching down at the same time as she reached for him, pulling him onto his side. Layne smelled the rain in the Drakensberg Mountains in South Africa where they had spent a whole morning sharing a sleeping bag, the pouring rain pounding the tent on all sides. She forgot about her hot coffee, her work problems, her out-of-the-blue text messages that spun her out, and concentrated on Rael.

"The neighbors," she said. For the first time, she noticed the blinds were open.

"Let them look," he answered, pulling her legs around him. "Concentrate on me, Layne. I'm here." The pressure of his hand on the small of her back focused her, and she pressed her lips into his chest.

Afterwards, Layne lay in Rael's arms and stared into his eyes. He didn't look away. He had told her he had worn an eye patch until he was ten years old because of one weak eye, and he had been teased in primary school. The "pirate" label stuck to him through middle grade and into high school. He had never been picked for sports teams, or even on the playground at recess. It was hard to picture that today as she ran her hands over his muscular body. It was important to him to stay fit, and the seed had been planted all those years ago, when he was left out of the boys' soccer games.

"I'll make one of my famous breakfasts. You can shower first," he said. "What do you have for muffins?"

"There are frozen blueberries in the back of the freezer. How did you know I was hungry?"

"We had so much to do last night, we never ate dinner," he said. He kissed her neck. "Don't tell me yogurt and a date count as dinner."

A forced numbness spread throughout Layne's body while she showered and dressed, leaving Rael to make his favorite spiced omelets and homemade muffins. But she could not keep her mind empty forever. Soon worries slipped in, and wound themselves around the front of her thoughts.

What did Layne think would happen when she appeared at her parents' house? The only thing that convinced her this was real was that someone paid for her ticket. Her family was so tight with money and always desperate for more.

It was impossible for her to believe that any trap they would come up with would cost them $200. It wasn't much for most people, but it might be the difference between filling up with gas and food for a week until they came up with another way to steal from moving vans, or fudge the numbers while running a cash register in some pop-up knickknack store. Her parents weren't picky; rip people off $200, $20,000 or $200,000, it made no difference.

Layne breathed deeply as she fought with her brush, trying to get it through her wet hair. She could not let Rael think she was such a horrible person that she would let her brother be institutionalized, without even a second thought. She would spend every minute with him this weekend and be back by Wednesday. She prayed for a sense of accomplishment and extra courage, even if she had to fake it.

The table was set for two. Rael had covered both of their plates to keep the eggs warm. Layne waited to eat until Rael finished his shower. She could smell the blueberry muffins baking in the toaster oven and congratulated herself on finding a boyfriend who could cook and bake. As someone who spent minimal time at home, the kitchen was not her forte.

Rael preferred to include herbs in his baking and have organic cheese muffins, but Layne didn't keep herbs in stock and her cheese was either cottage or cream. She would make it up to him and leave him with organic cheese and lots of echinacea and ginseng later. There were plenty of health food stores around here.

"Ready?" Rael said. He was fully dressed now in jeans and an olive-green sweater that suited his eyes.

"So, what will you do while I'm away?" Layne asked. She had devoured her omelet in two minutes, but he was eating slower, more on jet lag mode.

"Want me to ask Virginia if you can stay here until I get back?"

"Not sure her boyfriend would like that," Rael said. He pulled off the paper from his second muffin, even though the first one was only half eaten.

"Oh, he has his own house with a wife and kids."

"Ouch. Since when?"

Layne shrugged. "It's been official for a while. I have no idea how long before that. Can't keep track."

"Inappropriate."

Layne finished her coffee, wrapping her hands around the warm mug. "What's inappropriate?" she asked. "Virginia and her affair, or you staying here with her?"

Layne attempted to inject humor, but her voice sounded pinched. She consciously tried not to pass judgment on Virginia. Layne did not have the luxury of an abundance of friends, and even if she did, criticizing one's roommate felt like the initial step toward finding a new place to live.

"Her personal life isn't my business," Rael said. He took another bite of his muffin and took his time finishing it before he spoke. "Staying alone in an apartment with a woman is a bad idea. I've been around."

"I don't get it. Are you attracted to Virginia? Is this what you're trying to tell me?"

"I never said that."

"You implied it, and what does 'I've been around' mean? We've been apart eight months. Have you been around recently?"

Layne pushed her chair back from the table and closed her eyes. She reviewed the names of each student in her class, then began the list again, including their last names, until her anger disappeared. She counted the toothpicks in a jar on the table. She would not react.

"Hear me? I said sorry," Rael said. "That came out all wrong. I didn't mean it the way it sounded. It was a stupid thing to say when we've been separated for so long."

Rael put his hand on her knee, but she only looked at the floor. "Really, Layne, darling. Let's get back to the real topic and not this imaginary one. My brother's a stuck-up pain in the ass, but it's impossible for me to think we'd ever be estranged. What could have been so bad?"

Layne continued to stare at the floor, unable to meet his eyes, but she squeezed his hand. The idea of Rael with someone else while they were apart had occurred to her, of course, but she had always wiped the thought from her mind. Why did this feel as though he was trying to avoid her question?

"The truth is," Rael began, his voice tinged with a hint of vulnerability. "I don't want to be away from you so soon." He paused and searched Layne's face. "And it's time I met your family," Rael continued. He reached for Layne's hand, and she let him take it in his. "Why don't we both go and get Marvyn?" He let his words sink in. "Maybe he grew up. Maybe he's not what you think he is."

"Thought we had settled this," Layne said. She paced the room. The tension between them grew, and she hated that it was there at all, that she had allowed this.

"Guess not."

"If I wouldn't have forwarded you the texts, you would never have known. They would be in my trash box by now, and that would have been the end of it."

"But you did, and we don't have that kind of relationship, do we?"

Layne took a deep breath, and it hurt her chest to release it.

"Let's step out of this for a minute, okay?" Rael went to her, held her chin, and forced her to look into his eyes. She had to stretch her neck because he was a foot taller than her. "Step out with me. Not against me. With me."

Layne nodded with her eyes toward the floor.

"What does this feel like? Talking to me about your brother?"

Layne wanted distance between her and Rael, but he was still holding her chin, caressing her cheek with his thumb.

"You don't like the way it feels?" he asked.

Layne shook her head, and Rael let his hand drop, but remained kissing-distance from her.

"You're overwhelmed," he said. "We acted this out once before in a session."

"I wasn't expecting you to be here. I wasn't prepared," Layne said. She rubbed the back of her neck. "Now I have no job and I love teaching," she continued.

"I'm trying to hear you," Rael said. "I thought it would be romantic to surprise you, and it's better that I'm here to help you with this job mess. Much better than being across the world."

This was too much for Layne. Their first morning together shouldn't have been such a downer. Rael was right; he was very romantic to surprise her. She wished she had brought her phone to the table to distract herself and break their rule about scrolling while sharing a meal. That would have been the best thing. Then, the second-best thing happened: her phone rang.

Chapter 10

Layne hurried to answer her phone, grabbing it on the seventh ring after she found it half buried under the couch in the living room. The screen told her it was Parc and, for once, she smiled at his name.

Then she remembered it was Saturday morning, and her good feeling disappeared; weekends were off-limits for work calls. Parc was either asking her out again or, much worse, an image of Marco snapping photos of her came to her and made her want to throw up her breakfast.

"Sorry to interrupt your day off," Parc said. His voice was stiffer than usual, or Layne was already hearing the words he was holding back. She had been so excited to be with Rael, and so busy with their reunion that the pizza incident was pushed to the back of her mind. Marco loved her classes; he wrote her the nicest note only yesterday about what a great teacher she was. She could kick herself for tossing the message and the gift in the garbage. How could she be so stupid? Parc would have to take her word for it. Besides, what did those photos prove? That gravity exists, that objects fall to the ground.

"Not disturbing you, Layney?" Parc added.

"Of course, not, Parc. It's so nice to hear from you," Layne said. She made her voice light, ignored his version of her name, and convinced herself he was phoning because of her last text, or to flirt with her while he ate avocado and talked about testosterone production.

"Because I am a little disturbed. Do you know what I mean?"

"You got my message? I'm unexpectedly out of town for a few days and you saw that Rinata had no trouble covering for me. It's all taken care of." Layne counted to twelve and rushed into the hallway, careful not to slam the door behind her. It was too cold to go out on the balcony, and with Rael's eyes on her, she might lose control of her emotions. There were six people in the corridor; two had dogs, one was carrying cloth grocery bags, and the rest walked with their necks bent, sucked into their phones. The light was still broken, and there were cigarette butts overflowing in the ashtray by the elevator, even though it was a smoke-free building.

"I'm not phoning about your message."

Layne leaned against her front door. She strained to pay attention and ignore the comings and goings of her neighbors: the opening and closing of the elevator door; the ambulance siren outside; the construction work on the roof; or was that the pounding in her head?

Yearning to leap back in time to the life she had last week, Layne struggled to hold back tears of frustration. Parc cracked open a soda in the background and drank, smacking and licking his lips. Whoever told him women were turned on by his combination of phone calls and all the mouth sounds he can produce was either an idiot or a comedian.

"Did you open the online discussion board today?" Parc asked. He slurped through a straw.

"Haven't had a chance."

"That's too bad. There was a particularly interesting post with accompanying photos—of you."

Layne rubbed her eyes with one hand.

"The post wasn't so much interesting as damming. Know what I mean?" There was that annoying phrase again.

"Let me confirm the poster's name. Oh, here it is: Marco Monopolis. He even included a cute little video."

Layne wanted to crawl into the elevator and cut her cell connection with Parc. She did not want to hear anymore. It had finally happened. She could not pretend to be surprised. Every student and staff member had pored over those photographs by now.

"Do you want to tell me how Mr. Monopolis's possession ended up in the street?"

"Possession? Come on," Layne said. She picked up a take-out flyer from the hallway carpet and rolled it back and forth on the wall. "The whole thing was an accident. He left before he could accept my offer to pay, but I plan to."

Parc cleared his throat, cutting her off. "I'm afraid it's past that. He was fired from the delivery job and now he's lodged a formal complaint against you with the director."

"What? Fired for one dropped pizza?"

"It never really is only one thing, is it? The manager got tired of him reading secret codes hidden in the menu. I expect he was being paid under the table, he's not a citizen yet. Perhaps, they were looking for an excuse to get rid of him after some annoyed customer mentioned the heavily-accented and paranoid delivery boy. Why take the chance?"

Layne slid down the wall with her head in her hands. She shredded the flyer into confetti and made a tower out of the pieces.

"He slipped over the curb. Come on, give me a break."

"He said something about a twisted ankle, a hospital visit. Signed a document, too. You're lucky we make sure all of our students have medical insurance."

"That can't be true. He stomped off down the road." Layne never imagined Marco as a liar. But he had snuck out on the break.

"You were upset about your numbers and Marco was one of the students who left, sinking your class below the requirement."

There was a pause, and the sounds of ice clinking into Parc's glass reached her on the other end of the line. Coffee in the morning was too quiet for him. How she wanted to jump through the phone and strangle him for enjoying this, to ram her confetti tower into his throat.

"You think I was taking revenge?" Layne said. "You think I'm so petty that I'd try to get back at a student for dropping my class?"

"It's not such a stretch of the imagination and the whole thing isn't a good look, Layney. However, it so happens that after two years without a sick day, you deserve a small vacation. You see? I read your messages carefully."

Words roadblocked in her brain. She imagined one of those giant, mechanical arms that stop people from parking in private lots. She couldn't curse out Parc. He was still her boss.

"Rip the band aid off, Parc."

"You might want to consider your other options. I recall you spoke enthusiastically of finishing your MA."

"You're firing me?" Layne said. "Are you sure this isn't personal?"

"Personal how? I never thought of you as so emotional, Layney."

"Did you honestly just say that? Are you kidding me?" Parc did nothing but flirt and tease and try to get her into bed. It had been that way from day one.

"I'll speak to the director. You can't have final say on this." Her roommate was sleeping with the director, for heaven's sake. That had to count for something. He had to at least listen to her.

"James has given me full authority in this matter."

"I don't believe you."

"Check your email. You'll find two signed letters. One from James and the other from Marco. I suggest you think on it and if you're ready to compromise, you can come by my place and we can take a broader view of things."

"Do you really think this is how you'll get me into bed, Parc?"

"I have nothing to lose."

An incoming call cut Parc off, or he hung up, it was hard to be sure. Layne took a few deep breaths and massaged her temples. She estimated the number of steps from her apartment to the elevator and back twice.

Then Rael called to her. She let herself back inside where she found him lying on the couch with a compress over his eyes, muttering something about too much screen time on the flight.

"There you are," he said, holding up two fingers in a V.

"Two minutes and I'll feel better."

Layne would need more than two minutes to feel better. The heaviness of what had happened settled over her, and a voice in her head whispered this was a preview of what was to come. She should put the brakes on now, grab Rael, and get on a flight to anywhere else. The ground wasn't holding Layne. She collapsed next to Rael, her hands shaking as she adjusted his head so that it was in her lap.

Nervously, she smoothed the compress over his eyes, her movements overly deliberate. The neighbors blasted music through the walls, words in some incomprehensible language, further agitating her already tense state.

"Easy, easy," she said. She massaged his temples, his chin, his neck.

"Feels good," Rael said. "I'll be fine in a few minutes, but you don't have to stop. Any more texts from the mysterious Charlie?"

"Not recently. That was Virginia on the phone. She wanted to make sure she didn't disturb us if she came back a little early."

"A doll," Rael said. He took off the compress and stretched out, blinking for ten seconds at a time to moisten his eyes. Layne ached with irritation. When would she stop?

"The truth is, I got fired," Layne said, her voice shaky with anxiety. "That wasn't Virginia. It was Parc, the creep I used to work for." Layne collapsed in Rael's arms, and he held her, feeling the weight of her distress.

"This might just be a misunderstanding," he said. "Do you want to tell me what happened?"

Layne began with her last day at work: the disappearance of three students on the break and the note tossed into the garbage. She ended with the pizza splattered on the curb, Marco photographing her angry expression, and posting it for the whole college to see on her classroom site. There was no point in telling Rael about Parc and his invitation to his house—more like, his bed.

"I'm so sorry. I know how much you enjoyed your job," Rael said. Layne moaned and buried her face in her hands.

"I'm here," Rael said gently. "You're not alone, you know. When you get back, we'll start all over together."

"No more teaching for me."

"You don't know that," he said.

"Yes, I do," she said. Worry gripped her. "I'll get no reference for two years of work. I've messed things up and I loved teaching."

"You did not mess up. Things happen. Don't I always tell you we'll figure things out together? This too."

She gave Rael a soft kiss instead of responding and he kissed her back. There was no point in arguing with him, it wouldn't make her fears melt away.

"I'm glad you're here," she said. "Rest your eyes."

Then Layne shuffled into the kitchen, gathered their dirty breakfast dishes into the sink, and washed them. She moved on to wiping the table and sweeping the floor. When the kitchen was clean, she would phone Virginia and tell her what an amazingly cute handyman and cook Rael was, and talk her into letting him stay. It wouldn't be for long.

Layne knocked a bag of flour all over the counter that half landed in the sink, becoming a soggy paste. Bless Rael and his home cooking. The panic was here and she had to let it move through her. Her last paycheck might be in her bank account already.

The idea of those photos burned inside Layne's stomach. That was the first thing she had to do. There was no way Parc took time out of his precious weekend to get her off her own page so fast; surely, she could still delete anything posted. Any evidence had to go. She was fantasizing again, as though she could undo what had already been done.

Now Layne really had no excuse not to see Marvyn, and she had to admit, disappearing briefly had an appeal. She gave this whole story with her brother three days, and not an hour more.

Chapter 11

When no one responded to her knock, Layne didn't bother with the doorbell. It would have been disconnected in some way by her mother with a screwdriver or a hammer after her parents moved in. This was a mutual desire on the part of both of them. They discouraged visitors and not hearing them was an easy line of defense.

After another minute she assessed the absurdity of waiting for someone, who was supposedly not there, to let her in. Layne was certain Charlie would be here, but that was a mistake. Now, she hesitated to initiate a conversation with her, even by text. She yanked out her phone, stared at it, scrolled to Charlie's name and shoved the phone back into her carry-on. Charlie would not become her ally, even though it might help to have someone involved in the situation who wasn't Rael.

Layne could not fathom the idea of forming alliances in this town; she had already decided long ago that she would never make it her permanent home again. There were no footprints in the clean snow leading up to the front door for her to count, no sound or light coming from inside for her to evaluate. If they had a car parked outside the empty driveway, she would not recognize it. Neither of them had ever kept the same car for more than a year or two.

Maybe Charlie was lying that her parents had abandoned her brother, but even they would be home at 7 o'clock in the morning. Marvyn was another matter. He always came more alive at night than he ever had during the day, so it was no surprise he didn't answer the door at this hour, which was past his bedtime. Layne refused to acknowledge that like herself, her brother and parents might have changed in the last five years. She struggled extending the same benefit of the doubt to her family that she would to other people. Marvyn could go to bed on the dot at 10 p.m. these days, for all she knew. He might be religious about regular sunrise jogs and volunteer for the Red Cross.

Layne pressed on to the back of the house. There it was. The barbecue grill. Same broken appliance in a different location. In less than a minute, she found the spare key under the cover, which was all her parents' barbecue ever was—a key holder. Proof that she was right; no change here. The key was frozen between layers of ice and it took Layne a few minutes to break it out of its place and into her gloved hands. She suspected this would be the easiest task she would have during her stay. She returned to the front, hiked up the two steps—both caked with glassy ice and blinding snow—unlocked the door and entered her parents' house. Her parents moved as often as they changed cars, but it was the house at the address Charlie texted. This was something Layne had triple-checked before she exited the taxi.

Inside, the air was stale. The clock on the microwave flashed 7:00 in electronic blue. The microwave flashed 7:02 in red. In her heart, Layne was on automatic. Part of her brain was busy filling herself with as much numbness as she could create. She wouldn't let her mind leave her body. She wiggled her toes in her shoes and rubbed her hands together, keeping herself in the present.

True to Layne's expectations she saw a disheveled version of herself when she glanced in the mirror. She really looked like crap, a wishy-washy woman with smudged mascara and knotted hair. She shoved more of her thick hair under her hat, but some of it still peeked out. Her beyond-early flight was delayed due to weather or a technical malfunction, or some other announcement she only half heard. It was all she could do not to run back into Rael's open arms, and talk him into letting her ignore these ridiculous messages.

After spending two hours lounging out on three hard chairs, Layne had boarded. She spent an hour on a plane so small she could see the pilot. After that, she spent another thirty minutes finding someone to split a taxi with her all the way to Ottawa's West End, which was once called Nepean.

"Hello?" she said for no reason.

There was no sign of life: not the kettle when she put her naked hand on it, not the vents for the heat, not the water in the tap. So, no one was here recently. Score for Charlie. Layne drew an imaginary point on a phantom scoreboard in the air. She was already back in the game.

"Anybody home?" She cleared her throat and rubbed the rock she picked up off the airport runway between her thumb and forefinger, enjoying the feel of it on her cold skin.

This was another one of her old habits already back and settled in like a childhood allergy: scrap picking for good luck charms, more things to do with her hands. The glass kitchen table displayed her mother's stained romance novels and her father's free newspapers that looked as though they had all fallen into a wet sink and been left to dry.

An open cupboard door in the kitchen revealed several brands of bleach; bottles of floor cleaner with rusted bottoms that looked older than the floor itself; and furniture polish with ripped labels, all crammed into a space meant for a third of the items. Marvyn and disinfectant went together like hammers and nails. Nothing changes.

Layne bent and closed the cupboard door. It creaked against her palm. When she stood, there he was. She hardly had time to take a breath. Marvyn wore traditional blue jeans, a black GAP hoodie, and white Reeboks. His black hair was thick as ever, and minus the white streaks running through it, he could pass for sixteen instead of twenty-nine. His skin was the clear, glowing sand-colored hue his girlfriends' loved so much, and Layne would only know if he had any creases around his mouth or eyes if she could get him to smile.

Surely not yet, not before thirty. Right now, when his face was motionless, it was as smooth as any boy's; as smooth as she remembered her father's.

"You didn't beat the vultures, sis," Marvyn said. He smirked; the expression most natural to him.

"Are you still hanging out with vultures?" Layne answered. Her mind told her to run, but she planted her feet on the floor and crossed her arms over her chest. "More than ever."

"When will you learn?"

"I could ask you the same thing."

"I'm the one asking."

"You're here. You should have come straight to me."

Layne startled. A blast of cold hit her, forcing her out of her reverie. She squeezed her eyes shut and opened them. There was nobody here. The only Marvyn talking was the one in her head. She needed to verify what the real Marvyn was up to, so she could reassure herself he would never change, earn her brownie points with Rael as the good, kind-hearted girlfriend, and get the hell out of here.

Her therapist was the only person who had ever taken her seriously when she had described how real her memory flashes could be.

"Over here. There you are. The sister. Answer please. I've been so worried." Layne whirled around. Mrs. Volosovich had let herself in.

Chapter 12

"Mrs. Polina Volosovich," the old lady said. "But everyone calls me Baltica. You call me Baltica, too."

One hand rose to shake Layne's, but fell back at her side, as though she remembered Layne might have the same disease as her brother. Before Layne could chide herself for misreading the situation, Baltica had thrown her arms around her.

"I'm sorry about your parents, your brother. So, so sorry."

"Thank you," Layne said.

"Baltica," Mrs. Volosovich coaxed.

"Baltica," Layne said. The name stuck on her tongue.

"The street is not the same for me since this happened."

Layne gazed into the old lady's eyes, but they were hard to see behind scuba-lens glasses. She could not place the color. Why was this woman so emotional about her parents and her brother?

"Such good people, your parents," Baltica said.

"My parents?"

"Your brother fixed everything for me: my car, my toaster. And your mother used to fix my hair: dye, cut, and she wouldn't take money. I sent her so many friends from the bingo hall, they all loved her."

Layne eyed Baltica's hair, an inverted blonde bob, common in women her age. The color might be platinum or ash, Layne wouldn't know the difference, and neither would her mother.

"My mother? Dye and cut hair?"

There was no way her mother was a hairdresser, maybe Layne had come to the wrong place. There were no photographs up anywhere. Marvyn was a great fixer, but he was more into computers than anything else, and she had never known him to use that skill to help anyone other than himself. She was half-expecting this woman to tell her that her father had donated one of his kidneys to her cousin back in Moscow.

"Yes, of course. You didn't know your mother took up hairdressing? The magic touch." Baltica shook her head and put her hands on her hips. "In my day, children had obligations toward their parents. That's all gone now."

Layne opened her mouth to answer, but pretended to dig for something in her purse instead. She didn't owe this woman any explanations, even if her mother was her personal hairdresser. More like her personal con artist. Maybe she wore those glasses because she could hardly see, and her mother took advantage of it.

"Today children want to be understood and, if not," Baltica made a motion with her hands of a bird flying away, "obligations are out of fashion." Baltica's phone rang. "Excuse me."

Baltica spun around searching for her purse, finding it right by the front door. "Sorry," Baltica said into the receiver and slipped outside. Before Layne could get her bearings, Baltica was back. "Charlie's so stubborn. I told her you're here now. Not to come after her shift. He gets worse after she leaves, your brother."

"After what shift? Where does Charlie work?"

"She's a guard. Security."

"What sort of security?" Layne didn't know why asked; she could not care less. She couldn't get her mouth under control.

"Jail, you know. Prison. She'll get a good pension one day but it's a long way off."

"Isn't the nearest women's prison in Kingston?" Layne envisioned a place where women ate mush with sporks. She had to clear her head. Baltica either hadn't heard her or chose not to answer. Layne's head spun and she was short of breath. She forced herself to watch the hand on her watch for sixty seconds until she breathed normally.

Baltica's opinion of her was not her problem, she had to avoid a panic attack. She took deep breaths and focused on facts:

her parents were nowhere around, this neighbor thought she was the bad girl, and Charlie was texting her from a prison. She stepped back as Baltica moved closer to her.

"You're one of them all right with that wild hair. I knew you would come someday. I told them that. You had less than an hour to arrive by my clock. I almost gave up," Baltica said.

She continued to chat, but Layne was only waiting for her to finish.

"Have you heard from my parents? Either of them?" Layne asked when Baltica took a breath.

"I hear they have not been so lucky," Baltica said. "Maybe if you would have come sooner. But now, I don't know." Baltica opened her palms and raised her broad shoulders. Her face was a mask behind those giant glasses, and Layne was more lost than before.

"What do you mean 'not so lucky?'" Layne asked. "Did they call you; text?"

But Baltica only studied her nails, which Layne could only describe as floral fever with their wildflower design. If her mother had transformed into a manicurist also, Layne didn't want to know about it.

"You remind me of those socialwork people from the city, so many questions," she said. "They asked me everything twice, too."

Layne swallowed. She was unprepared for this, and she reached for the cold stone in her pocket, the tips of her fingers hitting each ridge.

"He might run if we leave him too long," Baltica said. Her feet were already facing the door. "Follow me."

"You don't have a number for them then?" Layne said.

Marvyn had never been much of a runner and Layne doubted he'd start now. The neighbor held up one hand, all five fingers patched purple-red with eczema that only enhanced the pink flowers on her green nails.

"I have the same numbers you do, but we must get going. My softy daughter has been begging to see him since he's been staying at my place for more days than I wish to reveal. She thinks the second she gets off work the first thing she should do is race over here and I told her no, but she'll soon get in her car. He needs his sister now, not more of what they get up to. That's not helping at all."

Charlie was Baltica's daughter? Maybe this wasn't a girlfriend Layne remembered. Before Layne could ask, Baltica was heading chin first toward the door, stomping down the two stairs in rubber-heeled boots with the company logo engraved on the outside. Layne could not find her coat. She had taken it off in the taxi and must have put it down when she was looking for the key. Perhaps near the barbecue. She buttoned her sweater as high as it could go. She would find her coat later. She pulled up her socks inside of her boots.

Layne hurried. She had a deep-rooted fear of strangers that she fought against in Toronto, but she was not in her adopted city this morning. With each step, the crunch of ice under her feet grew louder. Baltica had already disappeared into her own home, and her front door was shut; a leftover Christmas wreath welcomed visitors.

Layne tucked her hands inside the sleeves of her sweater and resisted the urge to turn around and taxi back to the airport. No, it was a longing—way more than an urge. She could not remember if she had closed her parents' door behind her and didn't want to check. She counted her steps.

Forward was the only direction if she didn't want to retreat and disappoint Rael; she must prove to him that he had found a Canadian girl much warmer and human than the weather. The person he spent his life with had to be suitable for Mr. Sunny South Africa, not jaded from the cold and ice.

Layne considered how she would react if someone else's brother was hiding out in this neighbor's home and this was all a giant mistake. She would feel ten feet tall; she would be free. What if her brother was off on a vacation with her parents, and a complete stranger had snuck into their home only last night and hadn't had time to mess the place up? Or one of Marvyn's ragtag friends had been staying there on invitation but worked eighteen-hour days, so he only showed up to sleep and leave?

Marvyn had always had a collection of hangers on, a squad of girly misfits, and odd-men-out types. He'd never thought twice about inviting them to stay on the couch, in the basement, Layne's bedroom, or the hallway if there were no free body-length spots.

Layne skidded on a patch of black ice and fell. The rock she had picked up in Toronto sailed out of her pocket. Damn. There was a small tear in the knee of her jeans where the denim had worn thin. She stared at the two tiny drops of blood for a second before she smeared them on her palm and then on the greying snow. She should have left it where it was.

Chapter 13

Baltica forced a window open and called to Layne. "You must hardly know where you are, it's taking you so long," Baltica said. Her smile was so large Layne sensed that's how she covered her insults: that and the flowery clothes and nails. "Come, come." Baltica aimed the phone in her left hand like a gun.

Even if there was a stranger in Baltica's basement, one of Marvyn's freaky friends, Layne could not turn back now. The cold had frozen the blood on Layne's knee to the spot. Her hands were already reddened from the wind. As Layne approached the front door, all she could think of was finding the stone she had picked up in Toronto before she boarded the plane.

A memory came to her. She was an eighth grader, covered in sweat, trying to hide in sleep because morning is where only Marvyn waits. What he wants to present to her is not a fist or a kick, but a story. One that would turn her world upside down and inside out again, and he could not keep it to himself another minute. They had to pack, run, and flee because something really bad had happened to one or both of her parents—arrest, bankruptcy, the details were unclear.

A new address awaited them, along with a new school, and a new car. However, all these 'new' things would turn out to be older and more dilapidated than what she was accustomed to. She had read about such situations in novels, where brothers play practical jokes on their younger siblings. However, Marvyn wasn't a practical joker; he took pleasure in being the bearer of serious news.

Then the backstory behind it—one Marvyn had time to embellish and decorate while she slept, so she never knew which parts were added or subtracted. This time, their father had been caught inflating receipts and there was no one to cover for him, or her mother was at the police station again for shoplifting lipstick, shampoo, or the latest, trendiest eyeliner. Marvyn's eyes would light up. How he admired the two of them. How he enjoyed watching her darkening facial expression as he devastated and frightened her, making her feel helpless and small. But she wasn't an eighth grader anymore.

The neighbor's front door was so light, she could not believe anyone could be trapped in there. Layne opened it without knocking, stepped inside and the wind blew it closed behind her. She jumped when it clicked and could not resist trying the handle to make sure she wasn't locked in. She exhaled when it turned.

"Did you forget something, darling?" Baltica asked.

"Sorry," Layne said. "Jet lag."

Baltica grunted with disbelief. Jet lag from an hour flight? Layne's embarrassment at her lie quickly turned to excitement. She was only a few steps away from the end of this ridiculousness. This would be over in a few minutes. There were fourteen daily flights between Ottawa and Toronto. She had been sure to check.

Rael's eyes, his hands, his lips, were waiting. Layne must tread softly. Keep this neighbor placated, so she did not phone anyone official. The house was overheated as so many Ottawa homes are in winter. Layne was happy now that she had not brought her coat. The smell of sour beets cooking on the stove was strong and the place was filled with faux plants and plastic flowers.

Layne didn't trust this woman and wouldn't meet her eyes as she searched for a mat to wipe her wet boots. She could not find one, but leaving a water trail through this stranger's home was rude and her boots were covered in browny slush. She found a rag in the corner and did the best she could with the wet mess. No more fussing over nonsense like a grade schooler. Layne needed to pluck her brother out of here, settle him with a trip to the grocery store if necessary and go home.

"There," Baltica said. She pointed a purple finger at the basement stairs and turned her back to Layne, stirring her cabbage. She wanted this to be over, too.

"No light for these stairs?" Layne answered.

"You're chatty," Baltica said.

The staircase was dark, but she could see a light on in the basement. The cabbage smell followed her down the stairs. She wanted to kill Rael for talking, downright seducing her, into this. Yes, she had been seduced several times. Still, she searched inside for his voice—the one that told her she was his now and her brother had no more power over her life. The only skeletons lived in her head.

It took a moment for Layne's eyes to adjust to the dim room. When they did, she saw him. Under an outdoor table. He was not even on a mattress or a blanket, but on the thinly-carpeted floor. There was no way of telling its color in this semi-darkness. Layne gasped. He was as she had imagined him in the kitchen when she arrived. He was wearing Levi's, a GAP hoodie and Reeboks. His eyes were closed and his face looked pained; his fingers clenched at his sides.

Layne approached her brother and kneeled. Marvyn was still scrupulously clean. There was no saliva at the corners of his mouth, no sleep in his eyes, stains on his clothes or odors of sweat or feet. There was nothing someone might expect from a person living under a table, refusing food and water. She saw comb tracks in his hair, only the five o'clock shadow on his face betrayed a lack of grooming.

"Marvyn?" she said. There was a tremble in her voice. His eyes flew open. Layne held her breath.

"Sis." It came out like the sound of water boiling in a pot. Sssss.

Layne was about to answer. Someone coughed. Baltica stood over both of them, an electric cigarette dangling out of the side of her mouth.

"Best not to startle him with light, darling, if you can manage it." Baltica had that smile again, but this time it was accompanied by tears in her eyes. "Your parents would be so happy you're here now," she said. She brought her hands together under her chin. "I'm sure they forgive you for taking off the way you did, deserting them. You're making up for it. A little, at least. I wish I could tell them myself or send them a photo, but I'm no good with these things." She waved her phone in the air.

Layne had to bite her tongue, so she wouldn't scream that this woman had no idea what her life was like or her parents. What lies had Baltica been fed? Layne needed repentance and this was it; she was redeeming herself. Layne would act the part, if it meant getting this over with.

There was dampness under Layne's armpits, on her upper lip. Her eyes darted around the room, but she could only make out silhouettes of objects. A vacuum cleaner, a pool table, a spare fridge. She could not be sure about anything with so little light in the windowless basement. She had lost track of time ever since she arrived at the airport in Toronto. It might be dinner time or bedtime, or the next day. Christ, being within breathing distance of her family messed with her head.

"Come on, Marvyn. Let's get out of here."

"They're gone, Sis," he said. "Split. After what you did, I was all alone."

"After what I did?" she said. She realized her mistake when Marvyn looked away and Baltica wrung her hands. "Shush. We're going to go home, eat and find them. I bet you would love that, right? Craving something? It's on me."

She stood, urged him to follow her with hand gestures because words were caught in her throat. There was a limit to her acting skills. She wouldn't go so far as to touch her brother.

"Are you listening, Mary? Gone, as in vamoose."

Layne sucked in both lips. She would not react to that nickname in front of this stranger. Mary was a name Marvyn used for naive people. She left her boyfriend alone after he'd flown from the other side of the world to tolerate her brother's childish, stale jibes.

"Okay, okay. You'll tell me all about it while we split a double cheese pizza with garlic bread. I'm seriously craving carbs."

Rael's voice came to her, but Layne could not imagine what he'd actually say right now, and there was a good reason for that. She had never spoken about her family.

The bad lighting made everything worse. Layne hurried through it, her boots clomping on the unfinished basement floor. She kept her eyes straight ahead, and maintained a normal pace. No running.

Chapter 14

Layne could hear Baltica's steady footsteps behind them and felt her record every word between them. She pictured a social worker, or worse, a police officer, taking Baltica's statement.

She considered what her own statement would sound like if she was forced to tell the truth to some government official. She could hear herself speak, putting on her English-teacher voice when she was reading a compelling article to her class, tossing in bits of drama: *In the shadowy corners of Marvyn Fortunefield's life, the absence of personal ownership and mundane responsibilities was not by chance. It was a calculated choice, a pact silently made with his parents and willingly adhered to, one I refused to join growing up.* Lane cleared her throat. The truth is no one ever offered her membership, it was always the three of them and her on the outside.

Cooking, laundry, household errands fell to Layne for as long as she was around to do them. From eighth grade, Marvyn existed in a perpetual twilight, sleeping all day, watching TV, or eating take-out pizzas at night, free from the obligations that tether others to the rhythm of the ordinary.

In exchange, Marvyn was at the beck and call of her parents, whatever they needed him to pick up once he was old enough to drive and before that on his bike. Marvyn was his parents' right-hand man: deliver forged rent checks or fake IDs; handle televisions that were merely choking on dust or unplugged for her father who posed as a repair man to a significant percentage of the city's senior citizens; race out of a restaurant driveway without squaring up the tab for their family lunch, there were so many things Marvyn was good at from a young age that her parents picked up on, until he met West Dicely.

Layne was a teenager when Marvyn met West and from the first moment, it was West this and West that. He idolized West, his first friend with his own car, and he could not get over the fact that people often asked if they were brothers. They even shared a birthday. The two went everywhere together: no one could get between them, her mother used to call them a matching set. They would spend their lives watching each other's backs and sharing a foot rest on the beach in their old age.

Within a few short years, dreams of sunny, sandy beaches soon dissolved into the reality of prisons and hospitals, but the three of them never spoke about that. The memory that hurt the most was the picture Marvyn's lawyer painted in the court room that day, one imprinted like a tattoo on her heart.

Layne had been sandwiched between her parents, barely able to breathe. Marvyn was in jail for ten months as the case dragged on. Already, he was a skeleton with huge eyes, and bony arms and legs. She hung on to every one of the lawyer's words. The same lawyer who had charged her parents' a fortune to represent Marvyn, money they did not have and could only acquire through shams of their own.

"West Dicely," the lawyer began. He looked larger than life, like his V-shaped body had waltzed off a screen in a double-breasted suit. Her parents were getting their money's worth, even if it wasn't theirs.

"West Dicely," the lawyer repeated and the name echoed around the room. "His hair permed, cut and dyed to match Marvyn Fortunefield's. In Marvyn Fortunefield's clothes, he waits his turn at Scotiabank and requests a withdrawal. He produces Mr. Fortunefield's driver's license, his social insurance card, hauling out $10,000 a week. A walk in the park.

"At twenty, Mr. Fortunefield thought he was about 100 times smarter than he really was, when he agreed to go into business with West Dicely and some fictitious relative of West's in the United States. They'd supply U.S. small businesses with whatever they needed: photocopy machines; paper; pens; ink; everything connected to office supplies at discount rates from his uncle's factory. Wholesale prices to beat the retailers. Business people placed orders from the United States that never arrived from over the Canadian border. Because there was no relative and no factory, only endless delays and supply interruptions. All of them are fictitious.

"Young Marvyn worshipped West Dicely, who could not keep his mouth shut about the millions that would pour into their accounts; the sports car Marvyn would cruise around in on his next birthday. The only thing that poured all over Marvyn was anger from irate customers, flowing like lava. Frustration quickly turned to threats and warnings. Small business owners, secretaries, bank managers hounding him, and when their patience ran out, policemen and lawyers.

"Barely out of his teens, naive Marvyn borrowed start-up money that West only used for fake IDs to impersonate Marvyn Fortunefield. By the time West left the country, there was not one document leading to West Dicely—who had been slinking around the U.S. signing orders as Marvyn Fortunefield for months. You have got the wrong guy."

Baltica's heavy breathing behind her brought Layne back to the present. She had to get her brother out before he said any more. She didn't stop to ask herself where this line of fear was coming from. When Layne reached the top of the stairs, Baltica crashed into her. Three steaming bowls of beet soup were on the table and the electric cigarette had disappeared. The V in Baltica's sweater showed off the tops of her large breasts and was short enough to reveal part of her stomach.

"A light," Baltica said. She pointed at Layne's parents' house. "A light switched on in there now."

"No, can't be," Layne said.

"Someone's snooping. Maybe another neighbor phoned, people hear things, and I'm sorry to say, but my Charlie loves to talk. There are meddlers everywhere."

"I might have left a light on," Layne said.

Baltica's expression said 'give me a break.' This woman didn't buy a word Layne said, not once. There was barking and Layne gazed out the kitchen window, where three German Shepherds snapped behind the fence. "Your parents loved them," Baltica said. "Especially your father. He had his own names for them."

It was all Layne could do not to roll her eyes. This was impossible to digest. Would Baltica tell her she named her dogs after her parents, maybe the youngest was called Marvyn?

"You want to borrow one in case someone's in there?" Baltica asked. Layne followed her eyes to a leash hanging on the wall by the door.

"No need," Layne said. She waved Baltica away. Perhaps her parents had returned.

"Suit yourself," Baltica said, but the way she looked at Layne told her that she was making a mistake.

Layne could not freak out now or worry about this woman's opinions. There was no one with handcuffs and an official document creeping around her parents' house, waiting to haul Marvyn away. It had barely been any time at all. Baltica's oversized glasses dropped around her neck and Layne saw that her eyes were black. It was her eyeshadow and mascara that were cobalt blue.

"Is something funny?" Baltica asked.

"Sorry?" Layne said. She glanced at Marvyn, who swayed.

"You're staring. Food is a better focus. Breakfast is ready."

"We can't," Layne said. "There's something about homemade soup, don't you think? Brightens a table."

"So sorry, but Marvyn needs to rest."

"All he does is rest. He's getting bony."

"Maybe another time," Layne said. There was a fourth bowl at the end of the table.

"That's Charlie's. I told you. She's bound to be on her way. Soft as a marshmallow. Fat like one, too."

"Well, send Charlie my regards."

Baltica's description of Charlie did not match her brother's preferred type, but that was years ago. Apparently before her mom became a hairdresser and her father a dog lover. This time, Layne stretched her arm out to steady him. Electric sparks flew through her when she touched her brother for the first time in years. The muscles tightened in her neck. It was static electricity. He had been rubbing against that thin carpet.

Layne guided her brother out the door before Baltica could say another word, walking at such a pace, she could pretend not to hear her. Baltica's eyes were on her back, and she straightened. Outside, Layne felt helpless, then comforted as she texted Rael.

Layne Fortunefield: Done. He's home.

Rael wasn't online, but he'd see it and respond. He always did. Rael would be pleased with her and that's what mattered, not all of those crazy comments of Baltica's about her abandoning her parents and obligations. That woman brimmed with delusions. She could hear the dogs' continuous rapid barking, warning of territorial invasions and other potential threats. Layne longed to give off the impression of normalcy to Baltica, but there was nothing normal about this. To hell with it. No officials were coming for Marvyn; if there had been any danger, it was over.

Layne felt as though she had won a prize, reminiscent of her childhood when she did not blink when she saw her mother get out of a police car, even when she was sure the neighbors could see. It was wiser not to turn around and express her feelings; Baltica had some nerve implying abandonment, and Marvyn was even more out of line for involving some person named Charlie to bring her here in the first place. However, speaking out would only prolong whatever awaited her. It seemed better to leave well enough alone, to adhere to what people had been asking her to do all her life: keep her mouth shut.

Chapter 15

Marvyn plodded along once they were in the open air. Layne slowed her pace to follow behind him, sick at the idea of his eyes on her back in addition to Baltica's.

She tasted the icy cold as they ambled down the neighbor's empty driveway, onto the sidewalk and back up the path into her parents' house. The heart of winter may have passed in other places, but not here, where it was the snowiest month of the year and bitterly cold, even with the weak sun shining behind the clouds that appeared out of nowhere. Toronto was only a few degrees warmer than Ottawa, and all the snow made winter here appear so much more intense. Layne had not been this cold in the five years since she had moved away. The freezing air filled her nostrils and throat down to her lungs and nipped at her ears.

Layne bit the insides of her cheeks to stop herself from urging her brother inside. She wished she could have left Marvyn in Baltica's house, but he wasn't some neighbor's responsibility. No one could be expected to house a grown man. She was tempted to steer him across the lawn, along the route she had taken on her way here with Baltica. Their twin tracks in the snow were still visible. For Marvyn, on the other hand, it would be impossible to know if he had been out of the house this morning. It was starting to sink into Layne's brain. That was the point. The thought made her heart pound. She had no idea what he was up to, and she didn't want anything to do with it.

Marvyn must have learned something in jail all those years ago, when he was locked up until his trial. He must have made friends and kept connections. She forced herself not to think these ridiculous thoughts that came straight from her past, a box she preferred to keep shut. The neighborhood was quiet, the only sound their footsteps crunching along the icy pavement, where salt pellets attached themselves to Layne's boots. Squirrels darted in and out of their hiding places, aggravating the dogs. Layne was grateful for the time to think. The sound of a car alarm or an ambulance siren would only add to the surreal feeling she was trying to shed.

Layne slammed the door Marvyn left open for her and wished she had taken the time to find her jacket. Through the kitchen window, the muted sky had transformed to a bright one, heavy with snow again. She had to go back outside before her jacket got soaked. She didn't plan on sticking around here long enough for it to dry.

Bracing herself against the cold, Layne opened the door. She trekked around the back, stepping in the same footprints she had made earlier. There, she found her jacket next to the broken barbecue. She picked up the oversized collar to cover her ears, and dug her hands into the wide side pockets.

Inside, she locked the front door. Then she thought better of it. She did not need a house key. This was her parents' house. She put the key on top of the fridge instead.

"You want to know what you're doing here?" Marvyn said.

Layne startled at her brother's dramatic change in tone. She could not tell how much stress he had been under, but this was a sign of something unsettling him. He had not said a word about her getting him out of the neighbor's basement, and she was beginning to think that she hadn't, that he could have stood and waltzed out of there anytime he wanted.

"I'll try to get to the point once you're a little more relaxed, Mary."

Layne forced herself to look away because she had her answer. She would ghost his provocations, and would not let him attach her emotions to a leash. His offers were portals to places she would not let him lead her.

Marvyn occupied the most comfortable chair at the kitchen table, the one with arm rests. He tried to hold his sister's hazel eyes with his black ones. The only feature they had in common was pointed out by Baltica. They both had uncontrollable black, curly hair, courtesy of both of her parents, who were often mistaken for brother and sister. Layne stared at her brother. She could slap him for calling her that ridiculous nickname; for dragging her here in the early morning hours; for stealing her away from the person she should be reuniting with.

Instead, she stuffed her hands in the pockets of her jacket and kept her facial expression neutral; the way she did when she was trying to control her class on a day they would not shut up.

"If you call me Mary one more time, I'm leaving," Layne said in her best teacher voice. "Got it?"

"Okay, teach," Marvyn said. "You're not some big mystery," he said. "I know where you live and that you're a teacher."

Layne did not hide her surprise well enough, or her pain. She was not a teacher anymore, at least that was her own private information. Right? A ridiculous thought. How could he?

"You even won some kind of award, didn't you?"

"It was an essay contest about teaching. CBC."

The Canadian Broadcasting Company was Canada's national broadcaster for radio and television, and held all kinds of annual contests. It was Parc who had entered her essay, without even telling her. She had written it for a staff meeting and he had praised her for days over it.

But with Parc, there was always an ulterior motive, and she had not let him take her out for dinner to celebrate. Or to breakfast, or lunch. Internally, gratitude welled up within her. Outwardly, she delivered a lecture on boundaries. Unsure if he caught the mismatch between her inner thoughts and external demeanor, she clung to the notion that she could skillfully veil her true feelings from him.

"Same thing," Marvyn said. "I also know who gave you that bracelet you're always twirling. It's from Johannesburg, no? Or, is it Cape Town?"

"This isn't a catch-up, Marvyn." Layne's fingers jumped to her wrist. "Let's deal with what's on the table, okay?"

"I said I wouldn't take up too much of your time."

Layne had no answer for that. She had wasted the first twenty years of her life, and she wasn't prepared to give her family one more minute, until yesterday. She stood, put her carry-on on the bottom stair, used the bathroom; washed her hands; and eyed her brother for the fifth time.

Marvyn hummed a television theme song and scrolled his phone. How Layne had admired him when they were kids, even as she feared his blotchy-faced aggression that could take a variety of forms. In particular, Marvyn took to hiding things she loved: her copies of *The Giver* and *Holes*; her Pogs and Beanie Babies; *Toy Story* phone cards. She could never locate her most prized possessions, whether they emerged from chip bags, were borrowed from a school library, or had been pilfered by her parents from a dollar store.

Layne learned not to get attached to objects. It would only mark them for disappearance if Marvyn spotted her love for them, and he always did. Sometimes, she would find her lost items deep under the dustiest parts of beds or couches. Other times, they vanished forever. Swallowed up.

Without thinking, Layne took off the white gold bracelet Rael gave her only last night. At the time, he promised there was a matching ring, one with a princess diamond attached to it. It was waiting for her when she returned. She held back a smile at the thought. Bringing her back to Marvyn, she snapped open her purse and buried the bracelet in her cosmetic case next to her tampons.

There was no way Marvyn would spot anything linked to Rael and snatch it from her. It was childish and pathetic hiding her bracelet, which she secretly thought of as her engagement bracelet, but she did it anyway.

Layne left the room then and lay down on the bed, taking deep breaths. Marvyn's whole demeanor was troubling her. He had always done this, but she was out of practice. One minute he spoke with the confidence of a salesman, and the next minute he was that crushed kid again, locked up behind bars.

"Do people eat standing in Toronto?" he called.

She exhaled and got off the bed. She returned to the kitchen, and he gestured to the chair beside him. She took the chair across from him; now they faced each other.

"Worried you'll catch something? Or are you alarmed about the light thing? There's nobody here. Baltica only sees real people on bingo nights."

Layne had forgotten about the neighbor's comment. If anything alarmed her, it was Marvyn, who disappeared into the bathroom before Layne could say anything. Her chair tottered back and forth, adding to her irritation.

Marvyn did not look the least bit thin. Indeed, she had never seen him so broad. She tried to look on the bright side of this. She would not have to spend time in an emergency room, or even a pharmacy. She snorted out loud at her self-deception. The promising side was quickly evaporating. Marvyn not only appeared well-fed, but far from skinny, indicating that both Baltica and Marvyn were liars. Her breath caught in her throat.

It was not the first time Layne had seen Marvyn's complete metamorphosis. When he was alone for more than a couple of days, he was like a caterpillar in a cocoon: no eating; frozen in place, his brain and body as animated as soup. Then, the minute someone expressed their concern, or offered to spend time with him, poof! He was his usual butterfly self.

"First things first," she said over her shoulder when her brother popped back into the kitchen. She would not show him how scared she was. She put on the expression she used on the first day of a new class, a well-practiced mask concealing the churning underneath.

Marvyn had changed into all navy: jeans, turtleneck and socks. He was freshly shaven and smelled like Head & Shoulders from the other side of the room. She had not heard him ascend upstairs.

"Food?" Layne asked.

"Not where you're looking."

Layne stopped shuffling through the fridge, which was full of things she would never want to eat: half empty cans of tuna with discolored edges; several open jars of mayonnaise; at least half a dozen open salad dressings; a super-sized chocolate syrup; carrots someone had already peeled, and bruised slices of green pears on side plates.

"I'm hungry," Layne said. She straightened. Her knees were sore from bending into the fridge. "Aren't you?"

"You're the guest," Marvyn said. "I'll do the necessary."

He clicked a pen and pulled a phone out of his back pocket. He clicked again as he scrolled. Layne counted the pens on the table. Ten Bic fineliners, another ten still in a package. The Fortunefields must be shoplifting from bulk stores these days.

"What are you doing?"

"Ordering in," Marvyn said. He continued to scroll on his phone. "Ventnor's? Notre Oriental? Little Atlantic has knockout Lobster Poutine."

"For breakfast?"

"Brunch." Layne shrugged.

Marvyn would order whatever he wanted them both to eat. It was only a matter of time before he asked for her credit card number. She gave it ninety seconds. She scrolled her own phone and kept an eye on her watch, while her brother filled in an online order.

"I'd treat you," Marvyn said. "But they don't take crypto, and all my currency's wrapped up in that right now."

"You can't be this predictable," Layne said. Her mind blanked on cryptocurrency. She had heard of it and it fit her picture of her brother.

"Did you slip any plane snacks into your bag? We could do plane leftovers for brunch if you don't want to pay and relax, Charlie will show up, she'll cover you. Plus, didn't you offer to pay at Baltica's house?"

"For a pizza, not lobster."

Layne held out her hand for Marvyn to pass her his phone. She punched in her credit card at the 80-second mark and made sure to press "don't save", so that he had no record of her credit card number. She slipped her card back into her wallet, returned to her phone, not waiting for a thank-you that wouldn't come.

Layne would never ask Charlie for a dime, yet the meal tab was far from the true dilemma. Somewhere along the way, a crucial piece was missing, and Layne was determined to track it down.

Chapter 16

Layne really was starving. She returned to her phone to pass the time until brunch was delivered. There was no point in talking to Marvyn before she had eaten. Distractions were not permitted. She could not slip up because of hunger. There were half a dozen heart emojis from Rael before he let her know his jet lag finally hit and he was planning to sleep for thirty-six hours.

There was nothing from Parc, but Virginia had shared a few awaiting bills. She calmed inside thinking she had two roommates now, two people who were big parts of her life, and forced herself not to think about her lost job. The apartment was not big enough for the three of them and it wasn't her style to live with her boyfriend and a roommate.

There was only so much overlap between her professional and private life that she could handle. Layne could not ditch Virginia, who had let her get behind on her rent more than once. Her mind could not process her new roommate situation. The food was taking too long, she had to start getting to the bottom of this now.

"The neighbor mentioned you haven't eaten for days," Layne said.

"Baltica seeks out dead bats," Marvyn said.

There was nothing between them on her end of the table. His end had stacks of novels and newspapers, but he made no move to organize them elsewhere. Marvyn's hands were behind his back.

"When she finds them, she keeps them in her freezer. The same place she keeps her beet soups." His voice was monotone, solemn. "There are people who get paid to test them for rabies." Marvyn whistled between his teeth. "There's a one percent chance, you know and the point is, good call on her breakfast."

Layne twisted her fingers together. She leaned forward and pushed her hair out of her eyes. "While we're waiting for brunch, do you want to tell me where Mom and Dad are?"

"I told you they're gone, didn't I?" Marvyn said.

"You did."

"So?"

Now it was his turn to learn forward, his hands clasped in front of him. "Let's be honest," Marvyn began. "You haven't seen them for how long?" He answered his own question. "Five years. That's 1,825 days."

He wagged his finger at her. "But you took off in September. It's February. Mary..." He paused on her name, and Layne smiled through closed lips. He didn't want her to leave, not yet. "It's safe to assume you don't care to see them again. Am I right?"

"This isn't about me," Layne said.

"It is now."

"Did you call the police?"

Marvyn burst out laughing and Layne's words sounded ridiculous to herself, too. Call the police on people who have spent their lives dodging and cursing the police; security guards; volunteers on patrol; anyone with any authority real or imagined? Call the police on a couple who entertain themselves bragging about their petty crimes and cons?

"If you're so fine with their disappearance, what am I doing here? Did I come all this way just to keep you from ending up—"

Layne stopped herself from finishing her sentence. She rolled a pen around on the table, enjoying the sound of plastic on metal. Then, she took the pen apart instead, rolling each piece on the table separately, careful not to get ink on her fingers. She had to reel it in, get control. Whatever was in the air around here was absorbing her like a paintbrush.

The table tempted her. Layne didn't care what Marvyn thought. She put her forehead on it and focused on the coolness of the wood. Varied temperatures were grounding, another thing she had learned in therapy. Temperatures and textures. Use the physical world, Layne. She put her palms flat on the wood, too. It worked.

"Well? Keep me from ending up what? You can say it," Marvyn said. "It's not your secret, is it?" He leaned across the table and rolled the pen out of her reach. "What do you remember?"

"It's not important. It's nobody's secret."

Layne examined her cuticles where they were red and puffy. Two got caught in the zipper of her case on the way here, and she had had to ask the stewardess for plasters. They still stung. She should have been more careful.

"What if I told you it was very important?"

There was a knock at the door. Their food had arrived. There was no one there when Marvyn opened up, only two large bags on the doorstep.

"Guess he wanted to get ahead of someone," Marvyn said, returning with an armful of takeout food in each hand.

It snowed in heavy streams now. There was nothing to see out the window but white. Marvyn slammed both bags on the table and tore open his. The smell of lobster filled the air. Layne had been starving, but now her appetite was non-existent. This whole thing stank. If she didn't get some answers this second, she would be in an Uber to the airport.

If Marvyn sensed her frustration, he ignored it. He shoved the novels and newspapers off the table onto the floor, then heaped food onto his plate, licking his fingers and smacking his lips. Garlic sauce spilled over the side of the plastic container, and he wiped the sides with his finger and stuck it in his mouth.

"Marvyn, whatever you were saying before..." she began.

"Yeah," he said between mouthfuls. "Something come to mind?"

She banged her fist on the table. "Where the hell are our parents? What were those bullshit messages from Charlie? Did they move back to Vancouver and this is one of your little protests? What does it have to do with me?"

Marvyn finished chewing. He wiped his mouth with the thin napkin from the takeaway bag. The way he watched her made her feel as though he was opening a door inside of her without permission and she inched her chair back.

"I get it that you're upset." He kept his eyes on hers and she had to force herself not to look away. "Those messages were not bullshit."

"You're neither starving, nor on the verge of being institutionalized."

"I needed them to get you here. Therefore, not bullshit. And the Vancouver idea is sharp. I'm sorry I didn't think of it before."

Marvyn returned his focus to his meal. He forked in his food in big gulps, talking with his mouth so full that Layne could not understand what he said next. Meanwhile, he waved around the salt, pepper, and garlic butter, adding it all to his food, mixing it around, and wiping his face with the already-used paper napkin. He ate better than Layne had ever seen him eat in her life. Charlie was right about one thing, he was starving. Butter dripped down the sides of his mouth and his lips glistened with sauce.

"Hold on." She raised her hand. "Before what?"

"Before I killed them."

Chapter 17

Layne's bare wrists stuck to the kitchen table. Spills on the surface had been left to dry for longer than she cared to guess. She had stained the sleeves of her shirt. She got up, looked around for a sponge and scrubbed around their plates when she finally found one. There was no dish soap.

Marvyn did not stop eating for a moment. Layne gave her brother her best bored face, the one she used to send Virginia the message that she must switch back to speaking in English, that she had worn out Layne's brain trying to understand her high-speed French.

Marvyn had lost his mind if he thought she would believe he killed their parents. He screamed when he saw a mosquito on the wall or an earwig on the stair. He would grab the nearest spray can and squirt in all directions until he gassed himself out of the room. Then, the room would be sealed, abandoned for twenty-four hours, and phone calls were made to confirm all was clear before he returned.

"You stopped talking to them way before I did, but I'm over that."

There was an edge in Marvyn's voice, not anger exactly; not revenge. He wanted something, but what could he want from her? Layne would not let Marvyn get to her. He had planted the same seed in the neighbor, who saw her as the selfish daughter who ran away. Fine with her.

Now that the table was halfway clean, she busied herself with her meal, trying to strategize. Unease crept up her spine, clouded her thoughts. She was nervous about her next move. She was unsure she cared anymore about her parents' actual whereabouts. She had not cared for years.

"You're taking this even better than I thought."

"Taking what?" Marvyn shrugged. "I thought you might freak out."

She bit the insides of her cheeks and cried out when she tasted blood.

"What exactly do you want?" she asked. Overwhelmed, she trudged to the sink and rinsed her mouth, spat blood mixed with saliva. "And where are our parents in real life, not in your imagination?"

"I see you're still confused," Marvyn said. "And having some comprehension problems for an English teacher." He shook his head. "And I really am touched that you came." He smiled at her as though he had won something this time, found a silver lining to wrap around her throat. His chair scraped the floor as he pushed it back. There were no crumbs left on his plate, not a drop of gravy.

"You want a story?"

"I want *the* story."

"Okay. Here goes. A terrible snowstorm hit a couple of weeks back," he said.

He paced, fiddled with the temperature control, then drew the curtains, leaving only the yellow glare from the single kitchen light.

Layne half-expected her brother would produce a candle or a Ouija board. She realized he was giving her what she expected and part of her was enjoying it. She hung on his every word like it used to be when she was a girl.

"I busted up the TV, so they could not watch the forecast and made a big deal out of a cross-border shopping day. You know how they loved to get U.S. deals?"

It was hard to take her eyes off of Marvyn's. She did not recall her parents shopping over the border, but her therapist mentioned once he thought she had dissociative childhood amnesia. Layne had not even bothered to look it up. She had dissociative everything else, so what was one more thing?

"Not much more to tell," Marvyn said.

"Except the murder part," Layne said.

Marvyn raised voice drew Layne's attention. "You know I'm the best mechanic in Ontario, probably in the country."

"You taught yourself how to fix computers."

"And bikes, cars, anything with wheels," he said.

"Of course. I remember now. They even talk about you in Toronto," Layne said.

Marvyn brought his hands together and clapped in delight. He was on the edge of his seat. "Car broke down when I wanted it to, in a typical winter blizzard." He put air quotes around "broke down," so she got it that he was lying. "Told them I'd get help. They could not see me stuffing the muffler with snow. There was so much of it falling, I brought goggles. It was an honest-to-god snow plague."

When Layne didn't speak, Marvyn snapped his fingers to a tune in his head only he could hear. Perhaps, the song that had been playing on the car radio at the time. As he searched for the right words, Layne could not help herself, and let his description carry her away. Images came to her. A mother and a father in an old, rusty car in a snowbank, hours from anywhere under a dark sky, they were all blinded by snow through every window, the music was on so low, it was only audible if you forgot to breathe.

"Carbon monoxide's quick and painless."

"Carbon monoxide." Her heart fluttered in her chest. "Poison."

Jesus. A chill crept down Lane's spine as the words hung in the air. Her eyes widened, and she blinked rapidly, trying to dispel the shock that threatened to settle in. The room seemed to blur around her as she clutched the edge of the table, fingers white-knuckled. She shook her head in subtle disbelief, her mind refusing to grasp the weight of the revelation.

In that moment, her gaze drifted into the distance, as if hoping the truth would dissipate like a mirage. Yet, deep down, a gnawing unease hinted at the realization she desperately refused to accept.

"I admit, it's nothing like five years of cutting people out of your life," he said.

"Well, we both didn't look back or say goodbye." She threw out that line to test him, but when all he did was stare directly back into her eyes.

Layne squeezed her own shut and struggled to stay in her body. She dashed to the fridge and yanked open the freezer door. Empty. Not a cube of ice. She opened the front door and shoved her hands into the snow, popped a handful into her mouth, begging the cold to keep her alert.

Safe in the present. Safe in the present. She ran back inside, her hands red from the cold. Marvyn was speaking on the phone when she returned. He rushed through his call when he saw her and hung up.

"Doesn't a coma come first? You know, once the poison's all settled in? You might have buried them alive, in the snow."

She watched his face, snow still melting in her mouth. Was he lying?

"Charlie said they deserved it," he said. "Double-crossers."

His voice came from deep within his gut. The cold pressed into her skin, as though she only now noticed she had been outside. She could not let him and his tall tales get to her. She would not. He must have invented this.

This narrative was an extension of the horror stories Marvyn spun to her when they were children. That was all. He had never grown up, not for a moment. If her mom was arrested for stealing a bottle of perfume, Marvyn stretched his arrest story out to include handcuffs and a beating.

Maybe her parents got frostbite and he had reinvented it to carbon monoxide poisoning. Jesus, she hated this. The truth was she did not know what to believe. If something criminal had happened to her parents, and she neglected to report it, she was an accomplice.

"They were out of here, they said. I could starve, right here, right under this table." It was his turn to bang his fist hard, and his plate flipped and clanked back down on the table. "They said they weren't interested in that old I'll-starve-myself move of mine. That's what they called it. A move. They had done what they could, they said, but it was time. Progressing, they called it and if I wasn't interested, it was fine with them. No one would come for me."

"You're long grown up," Layne said. "Are you telling me they wanted to retire in another city and you weren't interested in tagging along, so they left without you? This is ridiculous, you know that?"

The scolding teacher voice reappeared, but again she had lost control of the wheel. Every time she began to speak, her verbal foot was too heavy and she said too much. With Marvyn it was best to let him respond to one question at a time. If Marvyn was insulted, he hid it.

"A son is a sacred bond. Like best friends, or brother and sister. Don't you think? Doesn't everyone?" This time Marvyn stood and wagged a finger at her for the second time.

"A son is a sacred bond. Like best friends, or brother and sister, young lady."

It was her mother who always added the young lady part. How many times had Layne heard those lines come out of her parents' mouths?

It was like some private song between them. Layne met her brother's eyes and saw a face she no longer recognized. And why should she? People shouldn't change their appearance so drastically between twenty-four and twenty-nine, but he had.

Marvyn flashed a smile at her and drained a beer that appeared out of nowhere. Another change. Marvyn never drank and it was hardly one o'clock. He tilted his bottle as if to offer her one and she waved him off. There was enough adrenalin in her system, alcohol would not help her think straight.

Wait a minute. Part of Layne was stunned. Marvyn had performed an exact imitation of her father's voice alternating with her mother's. He had been posing for both of them. Did he do this only for her, or for others, like Charlie and Baltica?

Maybe that was where Baltica got her ideas about her parents. Layne had no idea. There was one thing she knew for sure: if her mother had transformed into a hairdresser and her father a dog lover, her brother had become an actor.

Chapter 18

The atmosphere in the room did not align with Layne's expectations. She anticipated anger and frustration, but not this cloak of mystery, and this sense of foreboding. Layne would do anything to be back in her apartment with Rael. She longed to vanish like a puff of smoke. She needed to shake off his story and excused herself, racing to the bathroom where she splashed water on her face and neck. Her parents kept a magazine rack in the bathroom long after most magazines went digital. There was one open on the counter. *"Unprecedented Antarctic Research: Ice Descent Experiment Sparks Curiosity Among Scientists at Taylor Glacier Borehole."*

Oh my god. A borehole. A deep, narrow hole in the ground to locate water or oil, but really anything could be dropped down into nothingness. Bodies, if the space allows. There are ways to make bodies smaller. Could Marvyn have dropped their parents down a borehole? There must be boreholes in Ontario, somewhere. How hard could it be to find one?

The video was shared on Twitter last month. It went viral, proving scientists have fun, too.

Marvyn dove over the deep end alone here with her parents, but to kill them? He would have loaded them into the car, knowing he'd return alone. He had left out that part, about the car. He would have had to dismantle it, hurl the remains into a deep part of the lake, piece by piece.

There were easily 250,000 lakes and over 100,000 kilometers of rivers in the province. He would have had to drug their parents to make them sleepy and driven into Quebec for all she knew. There were no shortage of lakes and rivers on the French side of the border. In that case, he would have needed to hitchhike back or take a bus. Yet, that would not suit Marvyn; he was not one to embrace unfamiliar company or gamble with chance.

She thought for another minute. Charlie the prison guard. She waited for him somewhere nearby. Kept the car running, so he could warm up between disposing of the bodies, then disposing of the car. He might have learned this in jail, back in the day. Charlie was someone he had met in jail. Delivering her parents to the border wouldn't take much. That could be true. He dropped them off on a "hey, we all need a cross-border shopping day," and didn't bother to pick them up. The murder part is a fiction for his own amusement.

Layne used the bathroom, flushed the toilet and washed her hands. It was only after she dried them on a towel that she read the hand soap label: *horse shampoo for radiant mane and tail.* She jumped back and a moan escaped her. Jesus Christ, she hated it here. Layne ran her hands under water again and dried them on the back of her jeans.

When Layne returned to the kitchen, Marvyn was gulping another beer with a woman she had never seen. They read some papers together, his hand over hers on the table. She had wide hips and a matching bust; a dimple in her chin; waist-length luscious blonde hair; and scuba-gear glasses like her mother's.

"You're here?" the woman, who Layne assumed was Charlie, said. She had a slight Russian accent and a superiority complex. "It's been so long. Marvyn talks about you all the time and of course, so did your parents. Welcome home."

Charlie kissed Layne on both cheeks, but Layne did not return the affection.

"It's hard to lose people out of the blue," Charlie said. "But for you it's not really out of the blue, is it? Considering you lived your life as if your parents were dead already."

Layne took a deep breath. Safe in the present, safe in the present, safe in the present. She wouldn't play tug of war with these two; let them cast her in the role of traitorous daughter, as long as she could figure out if she was really needed here. It was unsettling how they could condemn Layne for leaving her parents when she had never met Charlie in her life and hadn't seen her brother in years.

However, it would make sense to a warped mind like Marvyn's—a point of view he shared with his girlfriend. Layne noticed her brother's face filled with approval of Charlie, and a heart-shaped Marvyn necklace snuggled around his girlfriend's neck. It became apparent to Layne that she had been set up by the two of them to come here. Though unsure how Baltica was involved, Layne was determined to figure it out.

"What have you two been up to?" Charlie asked. She brushed back

Marvyn's curly hair from his face in much the same way Rael did to Layne.

"Joking around. Telling stories. We used to compete for the scariest story as kids, didn't we Layne?"

Layne shaded her eyes from the snowy glare streaming through the window. There were no curtains or blinds. She shifted from one foot to the other, not saying anything.

"Didn't we?" Marvyn repeated.

"Something like that," she answered. She played with a loose thread in her jeans. Charlie stubbed out her cigarette and lit another. She took a drag and the smoke curled up over her head. Layne would wait them out, until she could get upstairs and dig for any sign of her parents: recent mail; messages; clothes that smelled freshly washed; a computer she could get into, though that seemed far-fetched. She had to make sure there was nothing criminal going on, nothing that would get back to her for coming here.

Layne had noticed Baltica's cameras. They now had footage of her entering Baltica's house, walking out with Marvyn. It was not too farfetched to think that this footage would be used to involve her in something criminal Layne had nothing to do with.

Layne thought of her mother, Illiana, on a bench in Miami—a place Layne had never been.

Illiana had been planning on spending the winter there like all the Canadian snowbirds in February, and other than her wild tangle of hair, she would be as ordinary as any grandmother in a park. As overlooked as the fifth pocket in a pair of jeans. Illiana was not tall or short, fat or thin. There were no baggy granny dresses for her. Pantsuits for every season filled her closet, mostly in shades people wouldn't notice.

Her father, Pennard, was all hairy, skinny arms and legs in Bermuda shorts. Deep crow's feet circled his eyes from decades of refusing to wear sunglasses, and a distant look on his face, like nothing around him captured his attention. He could not rest on the bench for long, getting up often to stretch his legs that would only go from white to red in the sun and back to white.

Both of them would scout for prey, ideally, someone flipping through their wallet or parking a new car. Over the years, the connection binding Illiana and Pennard had only grown stronger, like tight threads from the same carpet. It would not take long for their eyes to gleam and glow over the same passerby.

Then Layne thought of Marvyn humming an old television sitcom tune that no one else remembered as he turned his back on the car filled with invisible poison. She tried on these stories like stiff new slippers, rocking each one back and forth in her mind.

Her therapist asked in one session, "Would you describe yourself as obsessive?" His eyes were so big; she wanted to jump into them, pull his lids down over her, and wrap herself in his long lashes. "Ritualistic?"

"More like alert," Layne answered. She leaned so far forward that she could smell the ginger-honey on his breath, reminiscent of Rael's favorite tea.

"How would you define 'alert?'" he inquired.

"Low risk. So many people get burned for not paying attention, you know?"

"Do you think you might not cope if you lowered your flag a little?" he asked. Layne let her head rest on the couch and circled the rim of her water glass until it hummed.

"Good question."

It was all she could do to keep her hands from touching his satiny hair. It was so black, even darker than her own. He had dark, coffee-grind skin to match, skin she was dying to caress, so she sat on her hands until they went numb.

Layne stretched her sweater at the neck where it was beginning to feel tight. Marvyn and Charlie looked at each other in the way close couples do, speaking with their eyes, their elbows, knees, and feet facing one another. One thing became clearer than ever: Layne's problems had only just begun.

Chapter 19

The light from her cell phone flashed, and Layne bolted up.

"Rael?" Layne said. "I miss you so much."

She was breathless and jittery from her dream. As she spoke, she touched her wrist, but it was naked and panic took over. It took her a minute to remember the bracelet was in its hiding place.

"Then you won't be angry with me?" Rael said.

"Should I be?" This was not what she wanted to hear from Rael; she could tell before he said the words.

"I missed the last thing," Layne said. "Sorry, I'm still waking up. You were saying?"

"I said something's not right, Layne. After you left, I could not stop thinking about how wrong this all felt. You haven't seen your family for so long, and you were so scared about those texts, and us being apart after only two days. Your job; the paranoid student."

Layne moaned. "It's too much."

"Well, let's try to take one thing at a time. I couldn't help it. I clicked on your links, and your password was automatic. I can't believe you pushed this guy. I have to be more careful around you." Rael's laugh was unconvincing.

"You're hilarious, and I did not push him," Layne said.

"That's not what I saw."

"You saw wrong. Give me a second."

She logged into the learning platform on her phone.

"Oh my god. These pictures are bogus. That is not me. I am telling you this is photoshop or something. Even in my dreams, I am not that tall."

"What do you mean? The date and time stamp are right there."

"Would I push someone? No. I cannot believe Marco would do this."

"Look, maybe it's the same photo from a different angle. Delete it again, hopefully Marco is tired of this. One other, small thing..."

"Rael," Layne swung her legs to the carpeted floor. She was wide awake examining those photos, and approaching high alert. She flicked on the light and blinked until her eyes adjusted. "How small?"

"I'm in Ottawa, out with your brother."

"Oh no, Rael." Layne hustled down the stairs, found her hand luggage, dragged it back up into the bathroom. The house was full of shadows. In Ottawa, it was dark by 4:30 in the afternoon in February.

"He's fine," Rael said. "You were right all along. This was a false emergency."

"We don't know what it is yet, do we?" Layne asked. The irony was not lost on her. They had changed places. Layne felt a twinge in her stomach. She dug through her toiletries for her toothbrush.

"I felt weird staying in a place with Virginia and you not around, and I took that as a sign to come find you. Rented a car, straight drive. You should cancel your flight back now and we'll drive back together."

"Oh no. You should have texted me," Layne said. She brushed her teeth with one hand and spat into the sink. It was as though a demon was sorting through her life, turning everything upside down. She had to escape.

"When I knocked, Charlie said you were sleeping. So we thought we'd let you rest, go get a beer. You don't mind, do you? I mean, I'm not stupid. I know you mind, but I'm hoping you'll put it in perspective. Now that you're up, I'll be there in half an hour."

Layne could not believe the words coming out of Rael's mouth. She tried to get her bearings. She was sure she had heard a phone ringing off the hook. It must have been the house phone, which she was amazed was still connected. The meaning of Rael's words sunk in. The exact opposite of what she wanted to happen, had already occurred. Not only had Rael met Marvyn, he met him unsupervised, with no one to guide the conversation. Hopefully, Charlie was busy sticking her tongue down Marvyn's throat. Baltica said she could not keep her hands off of him.

As disgusting as she found it, Layne prayed this was true. Marvyn loved an audience, and he delighted in taking away what was precious to her even more. Layne rubbed her eyes with one hand and held the phone with the other. She blinked back tears. This was a nightmare, no doubt about it.

"So, you're having a beer with my brother and Charlie at—"

Layne scanned her phone. Oh my god. She had slept all afternoon. Maybe she had taken sleeping pills to deal with the shock of what Marvyn had told her. Her therapist had prescribed them right from the beginning. "Six in the evening in town. And those photos are still up. Right. Am I caught up now? Anything else I should know?"

Though the house was warm and quiet, in Layne's heart there was only rain and thunder. The horror of her brother's story was something she could not unknow. She would be damned if Rael became an unknowing accomplice. He will never get to stay in the country if there is a shadow of suspicion on him, she thought, not to mention stay in their relationship. Why would he want to marry into an insane family?

"There's one more thing," Rael said. Layne's legs gave way. Her body sagged on the edge of the bed.

"What?"

"It's actually small this time."

"Oh phew, because thus far your confessions have been tiny," Layne wanted to lash out, throw the phone across the room in frustration.

"I've got you covered. If you're in pajamas, stay that way. And if you fell asleep in your clothes, take them off. I'm on my way to your place, but Marvyn and Charlie want to hang here for a while. I'd tell you where we are, but I don't even know."

"That's it?"

"What do you mean?"

"No, I mean. Okay, great. You're full of surprises lately."

Layne didn't want to hurt his feelings but she wished he had not come.

"You're not angry?"

"No, no." She thought throwing in a second 'no' might lend some credibility because in fact, she was very angry.

"Don't get out of that bed. I'm already in the car."

Before Layne could say anymore, Rael clicked off. She couldn't imagine where they were out drinking, but it didn't matter. What mattered was the three of them were together and god knows what was said.

Layne struggled not to cry. She had managed to keep Rael away from her family for years, and she passed out one time for a couple of hours and all that effort had dissolved down the drain.

If there was even a chance Marvyn and Rael hadn't spoken beyond the surface, she had to get Rael away from here. Layne reviewed the conversation in her head and could find no clue that Rael was unnerved about anything. She repeated this to herself until her shoulders relaxed. Rael was expecting her to be relieved that her brother was fine, convinced Marco would delete those photos, ready to have an intimate evening, and fly out in the morning.

There was no way Layne could leave without searching for her parents and working the phones: starting with cheap hotels, then the hospitals and finally, the police. She must make sure Marvyn was lying, so that her slate was clean. Police officers were not people she wanted in her life.

But Rael couldn't be here when she did or his chances of staying here will be ruined once his tourist visa runs out and now with no job, who knows when she'll have enough money to join him anywhere. Any normal person would run for his life rather than get involved with whatever Marvyn was cooking up with Charlie and she wanted an ordinary guy, an everyday relationship. She dug threw her purse, opened her sleeping pills and flushed them down the toilet. She would have to deal with her nerves on her own. No more naps. She had to make sure she stayed stronger and smarter and more alert.

Chapter 20

Changing her mind about a shower, Layne washed her face and dry shampooed her shoulder-length hair. She massaged the shampoo out of her hair and collapsed on the guest bed with her phone in her hand. Then she spent twenty minutes making a list of all of the hospitals and cheap hotels and phoned them one by one. It didn't take long to discover that no one related to Layne had checked in to either of those, at least not under a real name.

Instead of moving on to the police, she left her body. She felt floaty and her skin tingled. Her face went blank. The grounding snow outside was too far away. She had peppermint oil to smell in her purse that she used to stay calm, but she could not remember where her purse was. Layne didn't feel like an adult anymore, but more like an abandoned kindergartner.

She saw her mother on a visit to her paternal grandmother's house. It was more of an extended stay than a visit—one of many until her grandmother Atallie, died. She let her mind drift to the past. Every time they could not make the rent, the Fortunefields often ended up living at Atallie's home in Ottawa's wealthy east end, known as Rockcliffe Park. Sometimes it was a week and other times it was more than a month, even two.

"Your grandfather would never have forgiven your father," Atallie reminded her every visit, without fail. Then, she pulled out a prescription bottle of pills and poured herself a glass of water with two shaky hands. She downed one pill, then another. It was hard for Layne to tell how many.

"He's not a smart man: my son; your father." Atallie's voice was impassioned when she spoke about Layne's grandfather and their only son. Otherwise, she always sounded as though she had just woken up, or was about to doze off.

"He should have asked forgiveness before his father died, for choosing the life of a petty criminal and expecting us to bail him out every time, but he didn't. Now, he's even worse."

She shook her head from side to side and wagged her pointer finger at the same time. Then, she took another pill and another swallow of tap water. Layne saw her grandfather, with his trimmed beard, blue eyes, and the shadow of what was once a handsome face staring down at her father's tower of sins, burning with shame. She would give anything to distance herself from it.

Instead, it would become as much a part of her as an extra limb or a tail. She was certain that she had inherited her father's sins in the same way she had inherited his wild, curly hair. How could she grow up to be anything other than a liar and a petty thief deep down?

The dining room table served as her mother's makeshift office when they stayed with Atallie, but her mother was not at the table now. Instead, Marvyn sat there with a scowl on his face. His presence disoriented Layne, and her stomach twisted. She should warn her grandmother, scream, but there would be a price to pay for taking sides—more of her favorite things destroyed, broken, or sold.

It would be another catastrophic day for Layne, one wrapped in a ribbon of catastrophes. She had to disconnect, refuse to see events before they happened, as she often did in flashes. Above all, she could not witness events while they happened. She must never see what was really unfolding in front of her eyes. This is what she told her teenage self—her only shield.

"This isn't how a grandmother is supposed to behave," Marvyn growled in his father's voice. He grabbed Atallie 's pills and threw them on the floor. They scattered all over the dining room, and Marvyn crunched them beneath his shoes while her grandmother whimpered.

"Get away from me," Atallie said, but it was more of a squeak than a protest. Layne should have covered her ears, but froze instead. There was nothing to hold on to, not even herself; she was suspended in mid-air.

"Real grandparents take care of their grandchildren no matter what," Marvyn continued, his voice dripping with hate. A glass shattered to the floor from her grandmother's favorite set. If Marvyn could have, he would put the piece in an incinerator. Soon, only one glass remained.

"Think I can control your father? Think I can force him to get a normal job?"

"If you wanted to," Marvyn said. He stamped his foot for emphasis. "If you weren't so greedy."

His laughter made Layne feel sick. Everything Marvyn did to her grandmother was a warning to her. She was next. Even at a young age, she knew that.

"I said get away from me. Ow."

"He wouldn't have to do what he does if you weren't so, so, so greedy. Look at this place. What kind of selfish mother needs it all to herself? Sell it already."

"I'm saving it for you two." Atallie 's spike of panic was in her voice. "He'll blow every cent. My door is always open."

"Sacrilege, we need money now, today!" Marvyn exclaimed. "You could live to be a hundred. Are we meant to wait? Is nothing sacred? Your own flesh and blood."

"You're hurting me." There was a tremor in her voice, but it was obvious she had nothing to fight back with. Marvyn always won, at least until West came into his life, but that was still a couple of years away. Layne could not hear anymore. Her head was exploding, her stomach tight. She found herself upstairs, though she had no memory of getting there. Her door was locked. Half her body hung out the window. Her hands were on her ears, pressing them into her head, wishing she had never been born. Layne submitted to the weight of the memory.

Skipping a shower only made her feel worse, zapping her energy. Well, that was too bad. Old memories and low energy were no excuse. The search for her parents would begin this minute, while she was alone in the house. But already she heard a car pulling up in the driveway. She had hoped Rael would get stuck in traffic. How long had she been daydreaming about the past?

Layne had been in dark, confusing spaces before. It was hard gathering the courage to leave her parents and never look back, quitting her first degree, trying her luck in Toronto alone, and deleting her family.

Chapter 21

The street was lit up enough for Layne, her face pressed against the living room window, to spot Rael driving down the road and pulling into the driveway. Despite her heart beating in her throat, she smiled as the tires crunched into the snow outside. No matter what, when Rael was around, she felt better. She shook her head to bring herself back to reality. Maybe her parents were dead. There was no time to lose.

One look at Rael's sweet face, standing in the doorway watching him get out of his rental car, and Layne knew she was doing the right thing by sending him far away from here. This man would be her husband one day, hopefully very soon. He would not know the truth, but he would understand that this was not the time for romance; they would have all of their lives together. The thought made her smile. Mostly, Layne prayed for the right words to come to her in the next ten minutes, so that Rael would disappear without any consequences for their relationship.

"You should have stayed in Toronto," Layne said when Rael was close enough to hear. She could not help but laugh at how bundled up he was for winter. He had the whole winter works on: thick gloves, mile-long scarf, puffy ear muffs, and furry boots that reached his knees.

"I was worried you would be angry," Rael answered. "But if you're laughing, that's a good sign."

Layne extended her hand and beckoned for him to hurry inside. The wind whipped around her ears and was only getting stronger. The cold bit through her clothes. She could not wait to close the door. There was no need for Rael to tour the house, this place looked like a rental owned by anybody, certainly not by the proud parents of two children. If there was even a single photograph, it was in her parents' bedroom—a place she planned to go through thoroughly as soon as she was alone or Marvyn was asleep, whatever came first. She would have done it already if she hadn't swallowed those stupid pills. She was certain they were still fogging her thoughts.

"Aren't you going to show me around?" Rael asked, shrugging off his layers of clothing. "Hey, Layne, my darling. Come back to me. I'm here." Rael wrapped his arms around her and kissed her neck, her cheeks, her ears. "I know that look. Stay with me. Wherever you were, it's not what's real, I am."

Layne could not speak for a minute as she focused on Rael.

"I was thinking of my grandmother, you're right." Layne forced herself to meet Rael's eyes and smiled.

"I'm here with you now." She hugged Rael back and tried to feel his skin, but it was impossible with his thick sweater on over a turtleneck.

"We won't be alone for long," Layne said. "Come, let's talk in private." Layne locked the front door and led Rael upstairs to the guest room without turning on the stair light. She had kept the lights off downstairs too, except for the hall light. She didn't want to attract anyone to the house, including neighbors who might be thinking she craved leftover cabbage soup.

"You were busy with something," Rael said. He frowned. "You're dressed." He kissed her neck again. "Mmm you smell good, but I told you to wait for me in bed. Naked."

"Did you want me to stand at the door in the middle of winter naked?"

"Maybe," Rael said. "Preferable to wherever you sailed in your mind."

Layne winced. Sometimes she wished she could hide from Rael; he knew her too well.

"I'm here now. Stop worrying." Rael squeezed her waist, sliding his other hand under her sweater. He kissed her bare arm from her elbow to her wrist. "Meeting me at the door naked is not the worst idea you've ever had, even in this weather. Hey, where's the bracelet I gave you?"

Layne reached into her luggage and found it buried at the bottom. She took it out and let Rael put it on. It was a delicate, white gold chain-link bracelet, with their initials engraved on the clasp.

"That's better," he said, admiring it on her wrist. Layne whispered how much she loved him in Rael's ear. "We have eight months to make up for," Rael said. "One weekend was a good start."

Layne let Rael kiss her on the mouth and the pressure of his lips made her forget for a few minutes where she was and what she still had to face. But soon, all she could think of as she kissed him was that they might be in the house of one or more likely two murderers. She had to get him out of here. She fought with herself over her deceit.

"Mmm, we'll talk about everything tomorrow, and we'll have a good laugh, but now you've got to go."

"I told you I chatted with your brother, and everything's fine. He said I could crash here, too, if that's what you're worried about."

"Nobody chats with Marvyn," Layne said, her voice tinged with unease. She hesitated, avoiding eye contact with Rael.

"All right, chat was not the right word," Rael said, leaning back in his chair, completely relaxed. "He was mostly playing darts with himself, then we had a round of snooker, and that girlfriend of his won $100 bucks off me." Rael laughed. Layne could tell he was desperate to add a light-hearted touch to the conversation but she would have to disappoint him.

Layne raised her eyebrows. "One hundred dollars for a game?" she asked.

Rael smiled in embarrassment. "Two games. She was good." Another moment passed, filled with casual laughter.

"Gets a lot of practice in prison," Layne said, attempting humor but failing to mask the tension in the air. Another pause followed as Layne considered how much to reveal to Rael.

"Prison?" Rael questioned, his tone shifting from amusement to concern, realization dawning in his eyes.

Chapter 22

"I'll get you an extra strong coffee for the next drive," Layne said. "Or maybe you should stop at a drive-thru on the way out. I wouldn't trust the milk from here."

"The next what?"

"Drive."

"You're a big laugh," Rael said. "We'll go in the morning."

"I'm sorry, honey," Layne said. She placed her hands on his shoulders. "But my brother will be back any minute, and you can't be here when that happens."

Rael twisted his scarf around in his hands. The smile that had adorned his face was now absent.

"Yesterday's news. False alarm. Anyone can see the guy's fine."

Layne shook her head though she knew Rael's eyes were closed. "Maybe he missed you, or maybe you're right and he likes to pull weird shit. But there's nothing to worry about."

"You sound like me," Layne said. "Half a dozen theories for everything."

For a moment Layne was grateful Rael had yet to see her with her brother, and she wanted to keep it that way. She hated the idea of Rael seeing her around Marvyn. For her, his behavior, his mannerisms, and suspicions were contagious. Rael fluffed a pillow and settled on the bed with his hands under his neck.

"We can get a real night's sleep and head back tomorrow, and forget about it. You did the right thing, and see? It wasn't so bad at all. I'm proud of you and you should be proud of yourself. I'm sorry but after the five-hour drive and the beers, I have to sleep."

Rael pulled the covers higher and closed his eyes. In a second, he was snoring. Layne looked at Rael and wished it was that simple. There was a pain in her heart, a heaviness that spread through her. She let him sleep for a few minutes, enjoying the sight of him so close to her. She put her head on his chest and listened to his heart. She lifted his sweater and covered his stomach with gentle kisses.

"Come on," she said. She shook his shoulder this time.

"I really need you to go. I'll be back as soon as I can."

Rael opened his eyes. "You're serious?"

"Yes."

"You're wondering why your parents didn't tell anyone they were leaving? Is that it? The lights are on, the phone works, they're somewhere where you can go outside without freezing to death. It's common at their age."

"Good chance," Layne said. It was on the tip of her tongue to say that Charlie and Marvyn likely met in prison, a place Marvyn had spent enough time and that if anything bad had happened to her parents, there was no way Layne was willing to put Rael at risk. Not even if there was the tiniest chance.

She needed to know why her brother wanted her here and she wanted to find out alone, so that nothing would spill onto Rael. He must not be contaminated by them as she would forever be stained. A second theory came to her. All those people her parents ripped off. Someone was bound to want revenge. Why hadn't she thought of this before?

"You're overreacting," Rael said. "You're catastrophizing. You're the one who told me to point out when you do it."

"Maybe. Please, do this for me."

It was hard enough to immigrate to Canada without any blemishes on your record. There was no way they could close Canada off as a place to spend their future. That clerk in Pretoria had no mercy, none of them did. They had to be realistic. She needed time to figure out what Marvyn wanted and then they could put this behind them. Had Rael ever pretended to be loitering outside of a police station, when he was really waiting to take his mom home after she had been caught shoplifting from her best friend's clothing store? It was ridiculous to think her boyfriend would understand. The time to explain was over.

"Listen," Layne said. She switched the light on and Rael covered his eyes. "You have to get out of here. Now." She picked up Rael's clothes and organized them at the end of the bed. Rael stared at her, astonished.

"Let me get this straight. I drive five hours to see you, and seconds later, you're throwing me out?"

"Yes, come on. Marvyn and Charlie will be back any second and you can't be here. Trust me, please." She tugged at his arm, but he did not budge.

"Don't you think you've taken this my-family-is-crazy thing one step too far? Tons of people come from rough backgrounds and people grow up, even make up."

"Not this one. Please go. I won't stick around one second longer than I have to, but you're not part of this."

"But don't you see? I want to be part of everything. I'm not leaving you here, Layne."

"You are." Layne was yelling now and that startled them both into silence. Yelling was a rare occurrence for both of them. Time out. Time. Out.

Layne used the bathroom and showered, turning it on full blast. She breathed and paid attention to the air traveling through her body, her stomach, her legs. Rael had made the bed when she returned.

"Look, Marvyn may be delusional, good chance, and then I'll be right behind you." She put her hand on his arm. "Tomorrow even. But he may have gone off the deep end this time and you can't be involved in that. Don't you see?"

"No, I don't."

"There isn't more time. Leave. Please." Layne swallowed her frustration. He ignored her intuition about her own family and she had had enough. Her patience had moved from simmer to broil and her breathing exercise had gone out the window. This would be painful if her brother was here listening to them argue. She could not bear it. Layne took a deep breath and put her last weapon on the table.

"I mean it," Layne began. "If you don't leave, if you can't trust my judgement when it comes to my own family—when you already admitted I was right about coming here in the first place—then maybe we need to rethink a few things."

"What are you saying? Look at me."

"You heard me." Layne turned her back to Rael. Tears streamed down her face. She had never suggested they break up. They weren't one of those on again-off again couples. From the moment they met, they were on, he could not keep his hands off her. This was his fault. He was making this so hard, and she was only trying to protect him. She had only told him the bare minimum about her family and she wanted to keep it that way—forever.

"You can't mean this," Rael said. "I don't believe you want me to go. We've been working on these obsessions of yours. You looked as though you were in a deep sleep when you first came to the door. Didn't your therapist tell you to stop with those pills? Please let me stay with you."

He reached into his bag and took out a small bottle. "Himbah Myrrh from Namibia. My own recipe." He put the bottle on the only flat surface in the room, a side table. "It's way better than that peppermint junk you carry around."

"Now who is in denial? What does it take?" Layne said. "I'm trying to protect you. I have to protect you. Are you too stupid to see that?"

"Stupid? Stupid!"

"I didn't mean that."

"But you mean it when you tell me to go?"

Layne shoved her hair into a ponytail, took it out, put it back in. She blinked back tears.

"Fine. You know what? You know everything. I already chatted with your brother, and I wouldn't say he's average, but it was normal enough. Look, I could help you out here but have it your way," Rael said. "You've exhausted me. You've won."

"If you won't let me lead when it comes to my own family, this isn't going to work," Layne said.

"What isn't going to work?" Rael asked.

"This. Us."

"I hear you. Well, I believe in making joint decisions, so maybe you're right."

Layne kept her eyes closed, her face against the cold wall until she heard him stomp down the stairs, the jangle of his keys, the creak of the front door open and the slam of it closing. The window was dirty, but she pressed her face to it anyway. Rael hadn't taken the time to put on his winter jacket and all those accessories that had made her laugh only a short while ago. He unlocked his rental and threw in his bag, then he started the engine.

If Rael knew Layne was watching, he did not look up to the window. This hurt her even more. There was not a wave of goodbye or forgiveness. This had never happened before, and it felt like her whole world was collapsing. Something was terribly wrong, but there was no choice.

In another minute, Rael backed out of the driveway, and the lights flickered on and off in the house, warning her of the impending storm.

Chapter 23

The wall clock beside the window had stopped at 4:18 pm. It was hours off, and somehow that was like a brain magnet, an invitation for Layne to go even farther back in time. She remembered being thirteen, old enough to understand why she moved homes so often. Layne's mother was sunk into her favorite spot: the subtle taupe two-seater closest to the kitchen, her feet squeezed into zebra-patterned high heels that barely touch the carpeted floor. The rest of the couch wrapped around the longest of the living room walls.

If Layne stayed still, her mother would forget she was there and talk to herself. The words her mother spoke when she thought she was alone were some of the only words Layne ever believed. Layne held her breath and imagined a statue so hard, she became one.

Illiana licked milk chocolate off each finger, one by one, enjoying the potato peel smoothness of her artificial nails under her tongue, savoring it. She narrowed her eyes at the clock. Layne's father Pennard was late, and he'd always been the punctual one of the two of them.

"He knows tomorrow's delivery day," Illiana said to no one. "Suddenly, he can't tell time?"

She removed a wet wipe from a knock-off Chloé tote bag at her feet and rubbed it into her palms clockwise and then counterclockwise, as though she was polishing a charm. The hot chocolate she made for herself half an hour ago was murky, but Layne didn't dare ask if she could heat it up or drink it. The last thing she wanted to do was draw her mother's attention. The sweet drink tempted her on the glass coffee table next to the phone. The foam on the hot chocolate has evaporated. Illiana finished off another box of *Luxury 25+1* Chocolates. The '+1' was always a surprise. Layne hoped it was marble, so her mother would leave it for her. Her mother's favorite filling was sweet sesame.

"These letters and phone calls are making me crazy. Where the hell is your father?" Illiana jumped when the phone rang, her high heels sank into the rug as she lunged for the receiver. "This better be him. Not another crank call."

"Hello? Yes, this *is* C. Chest Accessories. I'm afraid not. The Leather Loft is not our only customer. I'm writing it down, Mrs. Tokenberg. Yes."

Eyes closed, Illiana wrote the name with her pointer finger in the air. She searched for the chocolate box and turned it over, banging the empty box on the coffee table, something that would upset her grandmother.

Layne struggled to breathe. She had heard this conversation dozens of times with numerous Mrs. Tokenbergs in the last couple of weeks since they had moved in with her grandmother, which her mother swore was temporary. Her mother's promises were no more valuable than the stickers Layne still traded up until last year in school. There was a click and Illiana let the receiver flop into her lap. After a minute the jarring beep forced her to hang up.

The April sky was grey and an unusually late snow fell. It was the powdery kind that disappeared before it hit the ground, not the kind that lasted. Then, her mother's voice imitated her father's.

"'You deal with the merchandising, and I'll do all the marketing, shipping and receiving,' he said." Illiana took a breath and when she spoke, her voice was back to its normal pitch. "Except there's zero shipping and zero receiving, because I'm marketing fairy dust to people and they're figuring it out way too early. Not according to plan."

Then, she picked up something—Layne could not remember, a vase; a glass—and hurled it against the wall, where it smashed to pieces. Then, the next object and the next. Smash. Smash. It wasn't hard to figure out who Marvyn was imitating.

Shaking, Layne screamed for a grandmother who was passed out on the couch; a plum-colored bruise on her forearm and a half empty bottle of pills in her hand. Layne was alone with a mother bent on smashing everything not tied to the floor. Anything could happen and she would be helpless in the face of it, nothing more than trash in the wind.

Chapter 24

Layne stretched for her phone and her finger hovered over Rael's number. But shame knocked her back. She threw him out; demanded he return to Toronto. She dropped her head in her hands and breathed in and out, then took two headache tablets with tap water after rewashing a glass twice. She ordered the largest damn pizza with the maximum number of toppings and extra cheese on some random local take-out app.

The wind howled outside, and the window panes rattled. Layne searched for the thermostat. It was baking in here, despite the icy cold. The place was overheated, like the furnace was on sizzle or broken, no one around to deal with basic upkeep. What Layne really craved was a heart-to-heart with Virginia, but this was the imaginary, compassionate Virginia in her mind. Not the real one back in Toronto: twirling her mini skirt at a party, head thrown back in laughter, wired on vodka straight up.

You're the queen of overthinking and stretching people to their limits, including the man you say you love so much. Why don't you try that sexy therapist again and if things don't work out with Rael, suggest more intense sessions. It's way overdue. You need a tune-up.

Layne had to concentrate: stop conducting imaginary conversations and feeling sorry for herself. She had time to comb through her parents' bedroom and confirm that she was not an accomplice to anything criminal, and she was wasting her time on this pathetic pity party.

Phoning the police was too scary a prospect for Layne. For now, the hospitals and cheap hotels were enough. A police inquiry would officially link her to whatever might have happened. She was not ready for that, and prayed it was something she could skip over. Her parents could waltz through the front door any second if

Marvyn was lying. Outside, the snow turned to hail, sounding like an overstuffed washing machine pounding on the roof.

Layne threw her shoulders back. It was time to get to work, so she could find some answers and return to her life. She would rather deal with Parc every day for the next year than be where she was now. She marched into her parents' bedroom and turned on the light. She blinked in the brightness. The screeching sound of tires. Flashing lights through the curtains. She raced to the window, and it was them.

Marvyn and Charlie were in the driveway talking inside a car, she did not know if it was hers or his. It was impossible to tell through the darkness if they were arguing, but they huddled close together. The streetlight was too weak to illuminate the driveway in a February storm and Layne's breath kept fogging the window.

She pulled herself away from the window to survey the room. A queen-sized bed with a white headboard was adorned with dull blue sheets. The room contained a white side table, a white wicker clothes hamper, and a long white dresser. Notably absent were any mirrors, makeup, or the usual accessories women often scatter around, no purses, pantyhose, shoes tossed into a corner, or scarves. Nor was there a master bathroom.

The walls were empty of photographs and pictures. The main feature was a corner desk with a computer blinking at her. There were two monitors an arm's length apart, a laptop next to it with a jumble of wires all plugged into an extension cord on the floor. The whole place screamed Ikea, rental and...Marvyn.

Layne raced out the open bedroom door and searched the whole floor. She was so stupid. She had no time and wasted what she had in the wrong room. But there were only two bedrooms; the guest room she found herself in, and this one that had been locked when she arrived. At least, she assumed it was a guest room. She double- checked. The cupboard was empty. There was nothing in the drawers. Nobody lived there. She ran back into the hallway. She could hear the creak of the front door and the slosh of wet boots on linoleum.

"Layne?" Marvyn said. His voice sounded far away. "What's with all these garbage bags? Did I leave them here? I swear being around you has cast a spell on me. We need to talk. Now. We're really out of time, sis."

It was all Layne could do not to go flying down the stairs, but she must not. She needed more time up here, she could sense it. She was still far from figuring this out. There was no way she could stop now. It was her last chance. She searched wildly around for another flight of stairs. Could there be a third floor, an attic bedroom? There were only walls and two bedrooms. Nothing more except a small bathroom in the hallway, one she was already familiar with. No, no and no. She swayed. Oh my god. She leaned against a wall for support.

"Layne? Your food's here. I paid for it, so we're even from breakfast. Hey, do you hear me? I see Rael's car's gone. That's good. Tell him to stay away."

"Why? Did you two talk about anything?" Layne said, but it sounded more like a cry.

"The vultures are circling. Come."

Layne startled. Marvyn had spoken to her about vultures this morning—only it had been a vision of Marvyn in her head.

"Vultures?" Layne called down the stairs.

"Are you deaf? These guys have claws. Get down here."

She dashed back into the main bedroom, pressed the keyboard, and the screen lit up. The background was a photo of Marvyn and Charlie, beers raised at Major's Hill Park, surrounded by thousands of tulips at Ottawa's annual tulip festival.

"Now," Marvyn shrieked, and the vultures continued to circle.

Chapter 25

Thud, clang, crash. A dozen garbage cans collided. The hair stood on the back of her neck. The wind rattled the windows. Was that one of those dogs growling next door? Layne prayed one of the neighbor's pets had come to play.

"You okay down there?" Layne called.

There was no answer from Marvyn. The silence bothered her more than the noise. Time was up. But Layne would not race down the stairs at Marvyn's command. She dawdled on the landing, weighing how she would confront her brother. Her confusion mushroomed with each step. Did the text message say she had to get to her *parents'* house? Her memory was cloudy.

And how could Marvyn pay rent on this place? She had never known him to have a job. Were landlords accepting crypto now? It was typical of her brother to claim money she could not see. Did her parents move to retire in Vancouver and forked out the money for a rental when Marvyn had a tantrum that ended up with him starving himself?

"I've been really patient up until now with this whole charade. But you had better be ready to talk up," Layne said, stomping down the hallway to the kitchen with her arms crossed over her chest. She raised her voice, so that it would be impossible for Marvyn not to hear her.

"I've had enough of this and if you don't spell out everything this minute, I swear, I'm out of—"

Layne was chilled to the bone. Marvyn was covered in blood.

Chapter 26

Never safe, never safe, never safe. Layne retreated into numbness to ice over what she saw. Marvyn's arm was in a sling, his shirt ripped at the shoulder, the scratches on his face looked like he was attacked by a cat, and he had one swollen eye. Her gaze moved to the blood-stained kitchen drawers, the blood smeared on the door, the ice pack on the table, also bloody. There was nowhere to hide in the world. Full stop.

If she was too stupid to have learned that lesson, then this was what she deserved. If she got clobbered into oblivion, she had no one to blame, but herself. Marvyn had murdered their parents, and there was only one person left, besides Charlie, who knew about it.

Her heart was beating too fast, and sweat gathered at the back of her neck. Her imagination moved into overdrive. She stepped back against the wall, and tripped over the stack of garbage bags she had made herself, falling face down on the kitchen floor. Marvyn reached toward her.

"No!" she screamed. "Stay away from me."

Layne struggled to remember the time; how close Rael might be to her, if there was any way he could turn back. He can read her mind, right? She could not think straight. She counted the scratches on Marvyn's face. Five. Like someone wanted to hurt him badly enough to leave a scar. This hand would have to be very strong, thick with sharp nails, at least one sharp nail that was full of Marvyn's skin right now.

"I'd muck in," Marvyn said. "But my scales are tipped. Wouldn't want any fall-out."

"Right." Layne scrambled to her feet.

"A towel if you don't mind," Marvyn said. His pain sounded strong. "You've discovered the bathroom."

"I have," Layne said, but only to herself. She could not tell if her brother was asking her a question or mocking her. Still, Marvyn's exhaustion filtered into his words. She had never seen her brother like this. He was no warrior, even as a kid he avoided school fights at all costs, and shunned group sports. She rifled around the bathroom cupboard, and found a couple of towels at the back.

"What happened to you?" Layne asked, handing him the towels.

"Special delivery warning as we were coming out of the bar." Marvyn said. He breathed heavily. "Tripping over this garbage didn't help. Do a triple drawer search. We each get a steak knife if he comes back unless you think I'm fucking around. Then you're on your own."

"Warning from who?"

"I'm entering a world of pain. Want to come? Give me a minute." Marvyn's expression told her he would need more than a minute. It hurt Layne to look at him. A honk came from outside where Charlie waited, but if Marvyn heard, he did not show it.

Then, the sound of tires screeching out of the driveway. That was not a waiting honk. That was Charlie hooting goodbye. Layne wanted to chase after her, beg her to come back, she did not want to be alone with her brother again. She had managed one meal and doubted she could manage another. If Baltica had let her dogs outside, they had gone back in. They would not hear anything either. The pounding of hail had stopped. It was silent except for Marvyn's breathing and the occasional crack of thunder that sent Layne into a cold sweat.

A far away bolt lit up an entire section of sky.

"Lightning bolts," Marvyn said. He raised his eyebrows but winced halfway. "The movie kind." Zigzags of lightning crossed the windows, increasing her panic. She told herself the facts: Marvyn was the master of creating situations that did not really exist. He did not kill anyone. He was not an actual murderer. Still, the lightning sounded like a message. In nature its presence means there is an imbalance of some kind between natural elements: cloud, sky, ground. Something was off.

"Are you still afraid of hospitals?" Layne asked.

"Charlie's as good as a doctor. Gets a lot of training at work. She cleaned me up, gave me something blue and something red, and it's taking the edge off," Marvyn said.

He stepped over to the kitchen sink and the way he wobbled, Layne understood Charlie gave him a strong pain killer. Marvyn ran the water and washed his hands and his arms up to his elbows. The metal sink turned dark red and Layne wondered if some of this blood belonged to the attacker. She shivered.

"Has the world gone crazy?" he said.

Layne raced upstairs and brought Marvyn a clean shirt. The towel was stained as red as the kitchen drawers and the door frame, but she could see now that he was no longer bleeding.

Layne smelled the pizza on the counter and the greasy cheesy stench mixed with the metallic odor of blood. The pizza top was flipped up, and she could see the canned mushrooms and bits of onion drowned in the cheese. She heaved and her mouth filled with spit.

"What the hell, Marvyn?" she said. "I can't believe someone beat you up like this. Something has gone crazy."

"West's signature," Marvyn said. He was beginning to slur his words. Bare-chested, he splashed water on his upper body, then dried it with the same towel. There was no more he could do with water, dish soap, and a towel not much bigger than a facecloth. He did everything one-handed. He threw his bloody, torn shirt in the garbage and held out his good arm for Layne to help him slip on his clean shirt. He collapsed into a chair and held an ice pack on his eye with his good hand. He winced and took it off, then put it back on, winced again.

"Can you believe that I thought you said West?" Layne said. "That guy who scammed you years ago." She forced herself to laugh. "I obviously need to relax."

"You don't believe in relaxing," Marvyn said. "Neither do I." He banged his fist on the table, but there was only a dull thud, he had no strength left. "West Dicely is back. You've shown up in time for fate. Mine and yours. Thought you would miss mine."

And like that, the rusty lock that should have stayed closed forever was cut open in the air between them, and the old pain resurfaced. Marvyn flinched and put the ice pack down. A purple-blue bruise had formed around his eye. His wild wet hair dripped all over the floor. Layne threw the towel in the puddle and then in the garbage.

"West Dicely." Layne ran out of words. She could not believe what she was hearing. It was too fantastical. Layne led Marvyn to the couch in the living room, holding his elbow to keep him steady. For the second time, she got an electric shock when she touched her brother. "Zapped," Layne said, rubbing her fingers.

Marvin stood there, half-asleep, attempting a feeble smile. Layne, her heart pounding with trepidation, assisted him in lying down. She hastily brought in a chair from the kitchen, perching anxiously on its edge as she kept a vigilant eye on her brother. Then, she meticulously ensured that all the doors and windows were securely locked and she double-checked to confirm both of their phones were fully charged. West Dicely was still out there.

It had been so long since Layne thought about West Dicely, she was unsure he was real. He was more like a cartoon villain from her youth. Her head spun with confusion and shame. Always shame, like ink stains in her blood. Her face was red with it, and already she could feel the hives coming out on her neck. The hives swelled into welts.

Marvyn snored on the couch. Memories flowed as she picked at the pizza in the kitchen. Her brother's scam all those years ago was not far off from the ones her own parents had tried to pull, only there was a major difference: Marvyn was not in on his own con, or if he was, he was too young and inexperienced to grasp what he was doing. Solid mentors in his life encouraged him in this line of deceit.

Marvyn was only twenty when he agreed to that stupid business with West Dicely. They sold office supplies to U.S. small businesses at discounted rates. The problem was the whole operation involved a fictitious relative, and nonexistent factory, so none of the orders were ever filled. It was Marvyn who took all of the anger and threats from customers calling to ask why their orders never showed.

Unsophisticated, simple Marvyn had borrowed money for the startup, which West used for who knows what? There were no supplies and no uncle offering them at a discount. Ultimately, West left the country, leaving Marvyn holding the bag.

Marvyn should have had internal antennas about con artists like West, built-in protection like an inoculation from her parents. Instead, the opposite happened. Her brother had fallen in love with someone just like Mom and Dad, and clung to him like a rope. No one loved West more than Marvyn, who was sucked into West's world like a magnet. Now, he was back, and he had Marvyn beat up. Impossible. Her heart was heavy with a mixture of sadness for her brother, and shame for herself.

Only moments ago, Layne entertained the idea that Marvyn would kill her, and stuff her in a garbage bag. Jesus Christ. She did not know what to think, she did not know what to think, she did not know what to think. It was all Layne could do not to snap.

Chapter 27

Layne was drowning in isolation; she needed to speak to someone. She left her phone charging in the socket, and pressed Virginia.

"What a coincidence," Virginia said. "Your man just knocked on the door."

Layne suppressed a moan. She was both grateful that he arrived safely, and that no one could see her misery.

"He did?"

"Poor baby looks like a wreck," Virginia said. "He mumbled something, and now he's disappeared into your room. What's going on?"

"Why should anything be going on?" Layne asked.

"Your night sucked, eh? My guy ditched me, too."

Layne could see Virginia's pout through the phone.

"You're not there with James?"

"I'm hands-free. Vacation, leave, family trouble? I could hardly hear him. That's guys, right? Listen, are you alright? You don't sound like yourself."

"No, it's just...my brother got beaten up." Layne could hardly believe she was speaking to Virginia about her brother. She had spoken more about Marvyn in the last twenty-four hours than in the last five years.

"Oh my god. It was a decision-fail, is that it? Rael driving out there?"

"Kind of."

"Are you at the hospital?" Virginia asked.

"No, he'll be okay," Layne said. "He's sleeping. It scared me and I wanted to talk to someone, and things got messed up with Rael."

"You worry about your brother. Rael can take care of himself. Look, next weekend, it's girls' time. I'll do your makeup."

"I don't want to burden you but—" Layne could hear Virginia hammering away on her phone, texting while they spoke. It distracted her.

"You're asking me to watch Rael? Let the women try to get near him. No one makes a move on your man. I got this."

In their shared apartment in Toronto, the doorbell rang, and Virginia hung up. Marvyn's cry pierced the silence of the night, startling Layne. Unsettled by the disturbance, she deliberated on her sleeping arrangement. If Marvyn turned out to be dangerous, would she be safer in the second bedroom upstairs? Or would it ease her mind to remain in the big chair, maintaining a watchful eye on him? Concluding that distance was key in dealing with potential threats, Layne tiptoed upstairs, terrified at the prospect of waking him.

After hours of struggling to keep her eyes open, Layne finally succumbed to sleep, gripped by anxiety that whoever had beaten up Marvyn might return to finish the job. The hard mattress was hurting her back and neck, yet she was too scared to sleep in the same room as her brother downstairs. Outside the bedroom windows, darkness surrounded the house.

Staring at the emptiness, Layne felt a strange familiarity. It was the same silence she had experienced during the jail visits, and later, during the hospital visits. It was the first time in five years she was in the same house as her brother. Maybe, instead of a predator, Marvyn was someone humiliated, embarrassed beyond belief at his own gullibility.

Yet, Layne could not afford to take that chance. She finally dozed off in the middle of the night to the sounds of snow plows clearing the roads before the early morning commuters got going.

Chapter 28

They were both yanked out of their dreams when Marvyn's phone alarm rang, and Charlie called at the same time. Twenty minutes later, Layne still had her blanket over her head, but it was already late according to Marvyn, who insisted they leave for the lawyer's office now, and assured her he would explain everything on the way.

Layne disliked how he was looking at her this morning, the uneven vibes he was giving off, like he was unsure whose side she was on. She agreed to pack and wait for his explanation in the car, but her hands shook as she tripped over her own underwear getting dressed.

She hated the way Baltica stared from her front step, and waved goodbye with her fingers when she stuck her head out the bedroom window for some air. Baltica had a know-it-all smile on her face, and three straining dogs on three leashes in one hand.

Without giving her a second to eat or zip up her boots, Marvyn urged Layne out the front door to the bottom of the driveway, where Charlie's car was already running. A candy-apple red Mazda 3: not the subtle escape car Layne expected from someone afraid of being watched. Her boots flopped open at the ankles, her half-zipped carry-on gripped in both hands, she slipped trying to keep up with him. February was yielding to March, an equally wet month.

The fog welcomed Layne as she opened the car door, attempting to avoid the below-zero weather. She enjoyed the notion of passing through the fog into the car, enveloped by clouds that had descended to the ground. It distracted her from her stiff neck and back, as well as her brother's watchful eyes, even if one was swollen.

Layne bent to zip up her boots and button her coat. She fastened her suitcase all the way around and placed it on the back seat, groaning at the pain in her neck from reaching over the passenger chair. The skin around Marvyn's eye was purple-bluish-black, and his eye was red. The scratches on his face still made Layne grimace. Today, they were dark red and deep. There would no doubt be a scar on one of his best features, his babyface.

"Are you sure you should be driving?" Layne asked.

"The fog will lift. We can't wait," Marvyn answered.

"I meant your arm."

"Charlie said it's a fracture, and there's no law against driving like this. Mom and Dad were supposed to be on a cruise for another couple of days, but Dad can't stop puking, so their return date was moved up."

"Wait. What did you say?" Layne demanded.

"Been hitting highs in crypto," Marvyn replied, a smirk playing on his lips. "They wouldn't turn down a free trip, even for a real estate deal. I bought them an early retirement present. It's community service, really."

Layne shook her head in disbelief. Nothing made sense. Marvyn, never a source of family kindness, had sent her parents on a cruise, all the while spinning tales of gassing them to death. He had become the worst, the absolute worst. It was a confounding reality that left Layne feeling like a dunce, unable to comprehend the drastic change in her brother.

"I had to get them out of town and you in town all in a tight window. I could not risk any blowouts between you that would send you running again."

Layne could not speak. This revelation was so far from the tale of luring her parents to a frozen lake to die in the car that her fury boiled within. Her father puking out his guts over a deck somewhere. Big brother Marvyn, the storyteller, and Little Layne always trying to decipher what was true and what it meant for her.

"Admit it," Marvyn said. His tone was mocking. "You love the drama, the possibility that one of us or, better, both of us will go over the edge, all the way to the end. That's why you were so keen to believe that story and you know it. It's in our DNA."

Layne was too upset to speak, but Marvyn did not appear to notice.

"Charlie left me her car, took her mother's lemon to work today. Mine's parked somewhere West will never find it. You forgot nothing, right? Got every piece of ID the government's ever given you?"

Layne pointed to her carry-on and waved her passport, driver's license, and birth certificate at him before she tucked them back in her travel pouch that she kept in the inside pocket of her winter coat. Her eyes still felt glued to her face. No sleep, no food, no coffee, and not one more word would she say to her brother. She would not provide him with another drop of ammunition to use against her. Questions swam in her head, starting with where the hell were they going and what the hell was happening, and could she possibly hate Marvyn more, but hell if she was asking them.

If Marvyn sensed her anger, he did not betray it here, as he had done so many times before. He was preoccupied with the fog lights, backing out of the icy driveway, Google maps, and the morning traffic report on the radio. Layne checked her phone to distract herself. There was nothing from Rael, not even an emoji. She could not decide if it was a good idea to initiate contact. She was too worn out to think straight. She texted Virginia instead.

Layne Fortunefield: Good morning. Hope Rael hasn't been too much trouble, ha ha. Home tonight.

Layne was not expecting an immediate response. Virginia took her time when it came to communication, and her parties ran late. Even if Virginia had to work, it would be a last-minute hungover rush with no time to check her phone. The traffic was heavy at 8 a.m. on a Tuesday and there were flashing light signs and cars as far as the eye could see. They passed a Starbucks on Greenbank Road and Layne rubbernecked the drive-thru.

"If I can't get a coffee, can I get an explanation?" Layne said, finally. "I damn well deserve one. Why in the world would you tell me, would you even imply that you murdered our parents when you sent them off on a cruise? I am such a dummy, so unbelievably stupid. I can't believe I did anything other than delete that text. Of all the things you've done to me—"

"Whoa, slow down. Teaching's made you soft. I already answered you. Don't you listen? Admit it, it was a rush for you too."

"A rush as in a thrill? You find this thrilling? This is what you get up to with your girlfriend?"

Marvyn laughed. "You can't escape genetics. You're as addicted to chaos as I am. You loved every minute of it. At least I'm honest about it. Now look, the issue right now isn't the parents, it's West. He already got it, and if we don't hustle, he's keeping the key to our inheritance," Marvyn said.

"Did anyone ever point out you have an annoying habit of starting from the end and speaking in code?" Layne asked.

"Always." Marvyn glared at the traffic and changed lanes. "I suppose I expect too much of you," he continued.

"What?"

"Follow," Marvyn ordered. "Don't go off like fucking lightning in your head. Ready?"

Layne switched off the radio, and ceased trying to defog her window from the inside with the back of her glove. She settled her hands in her lap, pulling off her gloves finger by finger, putting them back on, and stretching them over her wrists.

Inside, she seethed at her brother for concocting this murder story. He rattled her so much that she had to knock herself out for a couple of hours and order her boyfriend out of the house. Still, she could already feel the weight of what Marvyn was about to say and had to resist hiding her head in her arms, as if they were about to crash.

Chapter 29

"Atallie's mansion is ours, right?" Marvyn began.

Layne grunted in agreement. She did not question the mansion part. Things look big to kids. Her mouth was so dry. She popped open the glove compartment. No gum, no mints, nothing but a flashlight, duct tape, an emergency flare and WD-40. This was Charlie's car.

"Pinch yourself if you have to."

"Get on with it." Layne sat on her hands.

"This is the story of how badly you painted yourself into a corner."

There was a knot in Layne's stomach. She would not react. She would not scream about self-preservation at her brother. She would not talk about parents, who did not make one phone call or send one letter, except a plea for money in years. Vulnerability in her family was a sin, a stairway to hell.

"At twenty-one, you were supposed to sign and inherit, but you skipped town, refused to answer calls or acknowledge my existence. That's when I got into crypto trading." He pressed a button to roll down his window. "Choose a lane, jerk." Marvyn's hand moved to the horn, but hovered in place. He shifted in his seat. Understanding what Marvyn was telling her would require Layne to have x-ray vision. "Whatever you think Mom and Dad owe, you're way off. How long do you think they can keep it up for?"

"Forever," Layne answered.

Marvyn ignored her response. "They want that house sold and control of the money."

Layne felt hot in her heavy coat and gloves.

"I talked up that inheritance to West because he was the only one listening. Now, he shows up full of repentance, points Mom in the direction of that will."

"Dad agreed?" Layne asked.

"Surprised, Mary?"

Layne gripped the sides of the chair, ignoring the nickname. She could not refute it. If she had half a brain, she would have raced back here on her twenty-first birthday, and signed the inheritance papers the minute she crossed the city line, giving her parents zero time to get their claws on it. But she had always known her grandmother was clever, and she knew that Atallie would write a will her parents could not get around. Or at least, that is what she thought she knew. How old-fashioned, quaint, and absurd. She did not think they would turn on her so completely, leave her without a cent of security. Mary, Mary, Mary did not think.

"West still has the charm," Marvyn continued. His eyes kept darting from the side to the rearview mirror. "Said you abandoned the family for years, had given up your rights, that it would be easy to prove estrangement in court and he had the lawyer to do it. He gets this guy clients, takes a cut. He's been tagging us forever." Layne twisted under the seat belt. It felt so tight. She tugged at it, unbuttoned her coat, already her gloves were somewhere around her feet.

"Why would they listen to West of all people, after what he did?" Layne asked. She leaned in and adjusted the temperature controls. It was too hot in here.

"People like to reset their clocks," Marvyn said. He glanced at the GPS navigation system and cursed at the traffic. "He told them how sorry he was; this was the first step in making it up to them. He was desperate to show them a way they could get back all the money they spent on legal fees. How he was a kid, too; had no idea that's how it would go; his uncle made him do it. Blah,

blah, blah. Pick one. I stopped listening to their bullshit a long time ago."

Layne felt a jolt through her spine. Bullshit was a red flag word. Marvyn never openly defied her parents. Not the old Marvyn. Yesterday's Marvyn gloated about murdering them, and chugged a few beers over breakfast. After five years away, Layne was rusty. She sucked on her lips and prayed she could control her racing thoughts, or at least block them from shooting out her mouth.

Chapter 30

Layne switched her attention to the highway. It was remarkably snow-free given the storm yesterday, and there was only a thin veil of fog left. She added up the numbers in the license plate in front of her, and then the Honda Civic beside that one. Everything felt so alien. This city, this car, this story. It was like a glove she had to turn inside out to wear.

"I told them to go to hell. It was meant for us," Marvyn said. He tapped his fingers on the steering wheel. "West isn't working me over twice. They said you didn't give a damn if I lived or died, and I told them I'd prove that's not true. And I did."

"Those texts were a test?"

"Call it whatever you want. Here you are. But they would not give up the money idea once they had it. They'll be back in town by tonight, squeezes us a little. I'll be next door at Baltica's if they come sniffing around the house, and you know how much they hate dogs. They won't even come up the driveway if they're outside, then bye. Charlie and I vamoose."

Layne followed Marvyn's eyes in the rearview mirror, and noticed for the first time that he had his own suitcase back there. Marvyn had a got-you smile. He used it now. He turned off the highway. Soon they were in Ottawa's downtown on busy, upscale Albert Street. There were plenty of restaurants, hotels, and shops. Layne needed a very strong coffee and something warm and sweet: food she could sink her teeth into down to her gums, leave her stomach bloated.

"There's a café in the building," Marvyn said, reading her mind. "Caffeinate yourself and that signing shouldn't take long. I'll wait here and zip you to the airport."

"What about your arm, your eye?"

"West saw Rael's Toronto rental in the driveway. He figured it was you trying to beat him to the finish line. He's a wolf." Marvyn struggled to charge his phone with his bad hand. Layne did it for him, careful not to touch him.

"Our parents are back tonight from where?" Layne asked. Marvyn hit the dashboard with one hand.

"For someone who didn't give for five years, you're all questions. Who gives a shit? They're traitors, dead. Nothing's sacred to them. They've lost my loyalty for good. They never deserved it as it turns out."

"The carbon monoxide was a good one."

"You didn't call the cops?" Marvyn asked.

"No."

"Solid. Time's up," Marvyn snapped. He unlocked the doors with one flick, and pointed to the building with his chin.

"What will I say?" Layne asked. It was a stupid thing to ask him, but she needed to stall. She wanted as much information as she could get. "The less you say, the better. Sign and wave."

When Layne did not move, Marvyn unbuckled his seatbelt, reached over the back seat, and tossed her luggage at her.

"This is as easy as it gets. I'll circle around until you're done."

"Wait," Layne said, but she had run out of ideas. There was a pause between them. She caught her brother's eye and held it. She took in the dark stubble on his face, the nails on his hands were no longer perfectly clipped, one of his fingers looked swollen, like it got caught in a car door. She had not thought about what he was doing when he was attacked. Was he already in the driver's seat on his way home to speak to her, to save her inheritance? To save her. To save. Her.

"You're in an awful hurry," she said. She clutched her bags to her chest.

"These painkillers aren't extra strength," he said through clenched teeth.

"You're driving on painkillers?"

"Will you get the hell out of here?" he said. He smiled again, but only at the corners of his mouth.

"That was a very short explanation for a very big deal."

"There's no time for this and it's so simple." He moaned and hit the steering wheel. "West might do worse to me next, even if he doesn't go after you."

"A couple of days ago, I hadn't heard from you in years. I'm trying to understand and you're not letting me think. What about the sale? You're running it? And if West convinces Mom and Dad to contest the sale anyway?"

"They can't. It's a will. There are rules."

Marvyn's face was turning red, making his bruises even deeper shades of blue and purple.

"The value of the house will rise," Layne began. "We lived with grandma for a while. Mom and dad will claim some kind of possession; I can hear them already. You're doing fine moneywise as far as I can tell, and this is too ugly while Mom and Dad are alive. They'll never leave us alone if we come into that kind of money. The sale of the house will be contested, and tie us up for years until they get it all. We might as well just sell it, and hand them the money, and they'll lose it so fast; we'll be left with nothing. I'm not scared of West. You're letting the fallout from that attack run you."

Layne was breathless. She had emptied herself, stalling for time, thinking. A driver behind them beeped and yelled something in French out his window as he whizzed by.

"I could look into buying you out," she said before Marvyn could talk. "But this is crazy. When did you even have time to make this appointment?"

Marvyn glared at her and five years disappeared. Layne was thrown back in time. She noticed his clenched fist.

"Mr. Star won't wait all day." Marvyn paused after each word. "Are you brainy or brainwashed? That's the question and you don't know, do you?" Spit gathered at the corners of his mouth and one eye twitched. "Stop trying to defend the indefensible. You always do this sort of thing."

The air in the car had shifted. Lies had their own melodies, they were some of Layne's favorite tunes, the ones she heard the most often, that felt most like home. That house must be worth $3 million today. Maybe $4 million. Another honk.

"Get out of the way," a disembodied voice shrieked at them. Traffic swirled in both directions, motorcycles, cyclists. A mother pushing a baby carriage squeezed in front of their car and scurried to the other side of the street. The pressure in Layne's head made her ears pop. She rubbed them.

"West is a hitman who gets commissions from some random lawyer. Try the truth," Layne said. Now she had done it, used a family trigger word. Too bad; she was not backing down.

"Let's start at the beginning. Make it easy for you. Lesson one: grandma was an addict who slept in her own vomit, so we can't say how bulletproof her will was," Marvyn said. His gaze shifted from Layne to outside of the car, but Layne could not figure out what or who he was looking for.

"Addiction can happen to anyone," Layne said. Her voice was low, and she leaned back as far away from Marvyn as possible. "It's not a crime. And didn't you just say wills have rules?" A beat passed as Layne observed Marvyn's distant gaze, the weight of the words settling in the air.

It was on the tip of Layne's tongue to say she would never be as loyal to him as her grandmother, who never said a word about her bruises, and nobody ever asked. She talked to the pills instead or through them. Another beat followed, the silence between them pregnant with unspoken history.

"But I get it that you have to consider all options and by the way, grandma didn't cut you out," Layne continued. "She forgave you in life, gave you a second chance in her will." A moment of quiet contemplation lingered, a beat where Layne's words hung in the air, awaiting Marvyn's response.

"Forgave me? Lesson two. Sure, I was hard on her sometimes. That's how kids are."

"You were violent with her, Marvyn, an old lady, your own grandmother." Layne's words hung there, an unspoken plea for acknowledgment, for Marvyn to face the truth.

"You would put it that way. Someone had to fight for Dad's rights in those days," Marvyn said. "Stick up for him. I didn't know then he'd turn on me now." Layne took a beat to absorb Marvyn's justification, her eyes narrowing as she considered his perspective.

"She always let us stay with her in the hard times. Put a roof over our heads."

"Do you know how humiliating that must have been for Dad at the time? You're as ungrateful as she was." Marvyn's accusation lingered in the air, a beat of tension building between them.

"She was trying to protect the money from going down the toilet, so it would come to us." A moment passed as Layne spoke, and all at once Marvyn's expression changed, revealing a different side to him. It struck Layne that Marvyn was using his real-life, regular not-in-pain voice. Nothing like how he had been speaking until now.

Layne did not know if she was in her body or not. Had the conversation been real or imagined? A terrible thought occurred to her. Another beat, the weight of the revelation sinking in, before Layne could find her voice again.

"Look, lesson 3. That's ancient history. Today, we're on the same side. Dad ditched me, so that alliance is over. Now, we both want the money, and we both don't want our parents to get it. It's update time and I'll say it real slow: me, you, and grandma are all on the same side." Marvyn interrupted her thoughts. "So why aren't you running to sign? Cause you're overthinking again, that's why." This was real. Marvyn put his pointer finger to his temple, not unlike Marco had done.

"We could make it into two houses, rent them, and make more money," Layne said. She clutched her case like a shield in front of her chest. "Let's get professional advice."

"Why don't you do what I tell you and we'll both get what we want?" Layne did not blink.

"Okay."

Marvyn's shoulders lowered. He gave the guy behind him the finger in the rearview mirror.

"But before I do." Layne reached to the back, grabbed her purse, rested it on her luggage in her lap, and opened the door an inch. "Tell me, how much do you owe, Marvyn?" Her fingers gripped the door handle. "How badly do you need this money? Was it West you ran into last night, or someone you owe from last month? Does Charlie need it to get away from her mom?"

Marvyn's mouth hung open. His good eye flashed at her and his nostrils flared. She could smell the stench of something she could not identify in the car and wanted to puke out the window. Layne darted out of the way of Marvyn's arm before he shoved her out the door.

Chapter 31

Layne barely had a second to grab her luggage before Marvyn screeched off, almost cutting her fingers on the door. She turned and leaned against the glass wall of the building, her breath coming too quickly, her legs wobbling, her case rubbing against her leg like a shadow. Brewed coffee. Sugary croissants. Overheated air.

Someone flagged a taxi. Someone cried for her mom to wait up. Someone screamed into his phone. Mannequins stared flat-eyed, half-naked in store windows as they were dressed by women in skirts on their knees.

Layne wished she had never felt like she had to prove something to Rael. The way the bus driver smoking his pipe looked at her, she realized she had said that out loud, and hid her face in her hands, praying she would not turn into a puddle in the street. She could see herself flattened on the pavement like a massive gob of chewing gum, people treading over her arms and legs, taking bits of her away on the bottoms of their shoes.

The door to the café opened automatically. Inside, Marvyn's energy clung to her, his emotions were so strong they seeped into her bag, tucked between her teeth like floss, eventually they would bloat her stomach if she did not replace them with something else. Marvyn's anger, his threats, his fear, his blood all over him in a house that was not at all what she had thought it was. The floor began to meet the ceiling. She leaned against the only free table and eased herself into a chair. She had to hang on to herself.

"What can I get you?" The waitress was short, hassled, her hair still wet from her morning shower, one earring missing out of four.

"Large coffee, extra shot of espresso, the biggest croissant you've got with the most chocolate."

"Heartbreak breakfast, eh?" the waitress said. She smiled with her lips closed.

"Pardon?"

"Excuse me, a joke," the waitress said. "You don't look like someone who eats chocolate pastries too often."

Layne's phone buzzed before she could answer and she knew without looking that it would be a text from Marvyn, the Metamorphosis King. Let him wait. She put her phone on silent.

There were eighteen tables at the café, but seating for a dozen more if the stools at the coffee bar were thrown in. Layne was at the eighteenth table, the only one unoccupied and the only person with a carry-on. She considered this number lucky because when its two digits were added together, they equaled nine, coinciding with her birthday on the ninth day of the ninth month.

Her food arrived, and Layne ate on automatic. Recharged, she allowed the car scene to play in her head until her next step came to her. She ordered an apple pie this time, and let her thoughts flow. She grabbed her diary out of her purse. Writing always helped her order her thoughts. She flipped open to the next blank page.

It would be a bad idea to avoid this lawyer's meeting, and she must be prepared. She would take her time. Skipping out the backdoor and hopping a cab to the airport would not solve anything. Marvyn would hassle her in Toronto, it was not far enough.

She forced her attention back to her journal. Layne's journal, small but thick with 320 pages for scribbles and thoughts, rested in her purse beside her calm-your-thoughts peppermint spray. The journal exuded a faintly leathery odor, mingling with the refreshing wave of peppermint that enveloped her each time she opened it to write. The double shot espresso coffee would work its way through her body. It would take a while, but it would be worth it.

Marvyn had done something, and now it was her turn to respond—but it had to be the right response. With determination,

Layne busied herself writing down everything she could recall: every word Marvyn had uttered since their first encounter in Baltica's basement, if indeed that was the location.

Layne sipped, wrote what she saw around her, ate the apple pie, and sucked on the crust between her teeth. She had already left a message with the secretary that she was running behind when she felt more like she was running in place.

"Can I clear this away?" the waitress asked, her hair finally dry. It was a sunny day for a change and the sun beamed through the glass walls, catching the white gold on the waitress's finger. The engagement ring was delicate with a pear-shaped diamond and tiny chips all around the band. Layne stared at her hand so hard, the waitress noticed and showed it off.

"Congratulations," Layne said. "Stunning."

"That's my West. Premium taste, if you know what I mean."

Why couldn't the pain from Rael's absence vanish? Layne's misery was complete. Then she mentally replayed the waitress's words. Wait a second. West? She had no time to consider West. She needed a real plan before she faced this lawyer.

There was no choice but to reward her brother's behavior by signing on the sale of her grandmother's house, her only financial security. If she wanted to oversee the sale, she would have to stay in town for who knows how long, an unbearable option.

Her other option was to return to Toronto knowing Marvyn could not be trusted to give her the fifty percent she was owed. That is if he was wrong about her parents trying to get her grandmother declared incompetent when she wrote the will. Her last shred of security was up for grabs to the three least trustworthy people on the planet.

"Miss Fortunefield," the secretary instructed when Layne answered her phone. "Mr. Star has run out of time. You must come now."

Layne closed her diary with one finger and shuffled through her wallet, placing a tip under her dessert plate that exceeded the cost of her order. *The ring's not worth it and fake. If your West is West Dicely, run for your life,* she wrote on the serviette.

Grinding sounds came from the kitchen as she put one foot in front of the other, forcing herself to leave the café. All the way to the elevator Layne was followed by howling blenders, piercing oven timers, and the sharp sound of the bartender's knife slicing through flaming oranges, like small warning signals.

Chapter 32

Mr. Star had an energy Layne found penetrating. It was hard not to look at him: not to be hypnotized by his full cheeks, high arched eyebrows, and lips set close to his nose. All features she wanted to trace with her fingertips and then the palm of her hand, and her tongue. Then, there was the way he spoke; smooth, soothing, with his ego front and center.

"You've done well to come," Mr. Star said. He rubbed his hands together. "There's nothing to worry about, count on it. So nice to see you."

He stirred his black coffee from the wrist, then soundlessly rested it on the saucer. His intensity drew Layne's attention from his lips.

"You'll be so pleased with the outcome, I'm sure. The papers for the next stage will be drawn up and you'll be able to count on me for all of your questions." He stretched his hands over his head, and she saw the definition of his triceps through his tight shirt. His jacket hung over the back of his chair. It was Mr. Star's father who had befriended her grandmother, and he would keep his father's word; she could count on it. He did not favor one side over the other and was here to serve all parties to the will.

Each side should continue to meet with him separately, so there was no question of anyone signing under duress, particularly in this situation of uneven power relationships, Layne being the youngest family member. She was a separate client, as far as he was concerned. She could count on that, too.

Words were the only things that Layne might not be able to count, but certainly did count on. Words were everything. Then, Mr. Star cleared his throat like someone trying not to choke, and Layne slid to the edge of her seat, straightened. A shadow appeared over his feminine lips, and Layne flinched from the sudden cloudy look in his eyes. Whatever Mr. Star was about to say might sting.

Layne slid her hands under her so she would not cover her ears. She wished the words would burn up in his mouth, and leave him mute until she could get away. She should take out her bracelet and gag him like a hostage, fly out the window, climb down the building, roll down the street. Her mind soared off, and it was all she could do to drag it back to this office.

"I'm sorry to spring this on you," he said. All Layne heard was: 'run for your life' and her whole body tensed. "But Mr. and Mrs. Fortunefield appear to be in town."

"Of course, where else?"

A sigh of relief spread through her all the way to the ends of her wild hair. She had suspected Charlie was Marvyn's wife, a feeling she had at the base of her spine when she saw them together. She could see them circling the building holding hands, their eyes on all the exits, messaging Mr. Star to get a move on.

"Oh, you're expecting it? Good." He cleared his throat again. "They, Mr. and Mrs. Fortunefield, are waiting for you in the café downstairs. My secretary, she's new."

He bit the edge of his nails and pulled on his tie, picked up a pen, put it down, shuffled his papers. Layne was working up a sweat watching him.

"They phoned and she told them what time you were coming today. My sincerest apologies. I hope this doesn't cast doubt on our confidentiality. By the time I found out, it was too late. This slip is a one-off, you can count on that."

"Are you sure you don't mean Mr. Fortunefield as the other party? I hardly think marrying Charlie gives her a piece of my grandmother's home. He would have had her sign something about previous assets."

"Excuse me."

Thoughts braided together in Layne's mind. "Did Marvyn marry Charlie without my knowledge, is that it? Are they married? Don't worry about my feelings."

"Perhaps you misheard, Miss Fortunefield. The other party is not Marvyn, and I don't know who Charlie is."

Layne did not understand Mr. Star's expression. She needed to focus on what was right in front of her. She eyed his narrow shoulders and flat stomach. His long fingers, the wide wedding band. The coral and cappuccino rug folded over the back of the cool grey couch.

The whole time, he pointed at places for her to sign, initial, and add her social security number. Here, here, and here. They were having two meetings at once; their body movements mismatched to their words. "You said Mr. and Mrs. Fortunefield."

"Well, obviously, I meant your parents. Marvyn lost his share of the house back in...let me check." He rifled through his papers. "Four years ago, when he failed to complete two years of college by the age of twenty-five, a stipulation of the will. He was notified in writing several times."

"What?" Layne did not know what to do with herself. Her grandmother's voice spoke to her from the grave, and she strained to hear it. There was a stipulation about a degree in the will. Her grandmother must have hoped her grandchildren would go in another direction. Who could blame her? Marvyn lost his half of the house. Mr. Star crossed and uncrossed his legs. He had stopped pointing at places for her to sign, and spoke with his secretary on the phone in a language Layne could not understand. She waited for him to finish, her thoughts leaping.

"Did you really say my parents own half of my grandmother's house? Not my brother?"

"If Marvyn failed to meet the conditions of the will, your grandmother stipulated his portion go to her son, your father, if he was still living. This is something that you were notified about in writing, and you signed here that you understood."

Mr. Star slid a piece of paper across to her, but she did not bother looking at it. The signature was not hers. She did not need to see more of her parents' artwork. "You've brought copies of your degree?"

"I could access it in my employee file on the school's learning program and forward it to you."

"You're very resourceful, Miss Fortunefield. Must be a good teacher."

"You said my parents are here?"

But Layne failed to register Mr. Star's response. The air around her thickened. It was not as easy to breathe as it was before. Then, Layne was gone. A feeling of descent ran through her. She was dropping, sailing down two floors, three, five, seven, nine. She landed and gripped the chair. The landing let the nausea drain, at least that.

Where was she? Things were blurry as the part of her mind in control struggled to decide on a location. She half-saw a park, half-saw nothing. She was nowhere. This place was a freefall zone she now recognized like a dirty public bathroom, an airplane toilet, or the back of the bus, somewhere people go who don't want to be there. That's where she was. Alone.

Layne leaned back in her armchair that was designed for someone much taller than her five feet. Her legs dangled, and she had to hold her spine straight so as not to slump. This did not bring her back into her body, there was not enough contact, everything in this office was temperature controlled. The freefall zone swallowed her and made it difficult to hold one complete thought. Words slipped through her mind, and were gone faster than she could get a grip on them.

"Miss Fortunefield? Layne," Mr. Star said. "We're about out of time, but something to drink on your way out?"

Layne heard his voice from far away, on low resolution. She was in a cold sweat, and could not hold the memory back. These were the worst kind of dissociations, a voice in her head told her.

There were so many parts of her brain working, it was like being awake in a dream. Layne would remember and dissociate at the same time. Like a stuffed doll, she embraced it because she was not controlling her arms and legs, her mouth filling with spit and drying out, filling and drying, her body a laundry mat, making her stomach heave.

Seventeen-year-old Layne grabbed the largest suitcase and threw it open on her bed. They had only just moved to this house. Layne could not count the moves anymore, but it made the packing easy. Between her brother disposing of her favorite possessions, and her parents' frequent moves, she owned next to nothing. Her heart sang: she was getting out. She would be free for the first time ever. But even freedom took strength. Layne scurried upstairs to grab her running shoes from the front closet, but did not escape her mother's eyes.

"What are you doing?" Illiana screamed.

"Moving." Layne had nothing to say to her. She was a ball of emotion and there was so much rage and hatred inside of her, there was not enough space for it all. This woman had never protected her from anything.

"Are you trying to embarrass me in front of your grandmother?" Illiana shrieked.

Layne glanced at Illiana, her anger evident in the tight clench of her jaw and the fiery intensity in her eyes.

"You would do this to me," Illiana spat, her tone seething with frustration.

Layne stopped herself from speaking by sucking in her cheeks and hauled her two suitcases up the stairs, through the kitchen, and onto the driveway. She screeched away in a cab, the grating sound her only goodbye.

The memory twisted and the cab surged ahead until Layne realized that it was not a freedom cab at all, it was another trap. The windows were either painted black, or it was the middle of the night under a moonless sky, where the stars had abandoned her. One way or the other, she was blind and had taken control of a cab that had no brakes on a road without end. She felt so stupid, a recurring theme in many of her dissociations. She thought she was escaping, but instead, she was only trading one prison for another. Now, she was trapped and feeling stupid.

Horror swept over Layne as she realized the windows and door were locked. It was only a matter of time before she ran out of air or ran out of road, with not a soul around to save her.

Chapter 33

"Please drink," Mr. Star said. Ice clinked in a glass, snapping her back into the chair. "Have some water, eh? You must be exhausted. Did you drive here alone? Another coffee?"

"No, I took the train from Toronto," Layne lied, reaching for the water. Mr. Star's voice was feathery. Was this the voice he used when he wanted people to trust him? She felt a pang of jealousy. Others were in a much better headspace, and she wanted into that zone.

Layne gripped the glass of water and sipped. She concentrated on the feeling of her lips on the cold glass; her tongue on the ice cubes; at the back of her mouth. Seventy-three, seventy-three, seventy-three. No, ten, ten, ten. No. Eight, sixteen, twenty-four.

It was unbelievably bright in here, and how can anyone work with all of those busses bleating down the road every second? All Layne needed was for a phone to go off with some ringtone she could not stand to listen to for more than three seconds.

"You're even whiter than usual. Count on this winter weather, eh? Warmer in Toronto. We really do need to wrap up."

"Wrap up?" Layne was still breathless from her dissociation. "Sneak me out in your briefcase."

"You have a good sense of humor, Miss Fortunefield. If you could show me that degree."

The honey in Mr. Star's voice made Layne want to run. In her experience, sweet was usually followed by something sour. She accessed the school's online system on her phone and her personal profile. She forwarded the copy of her BA to Mr. Star. No one said anything while they waited for it to arrive in his inbox. There was only the tap, tap, tap of Mr. Star's fingers on his desk. The rhythmic tapping helped Layne put things together.

Marvyn had been conned by her parents. She was not sure precisely how, forging his signature on a letter that said he understood the conditions of the will? It was exhausting to get into their heads, to watch their every move, habits she had never broken while she lived with them.

Mr. Star held out his hand and leaned forward, expanding his collar in his loose shirt. Layne shook the ends of his fingers, noticing the scratches on his neck. Someone angry had run thorns along his skin, or someone passionate had sharp nails. His eyes followed hers.

"My wife has a thing. First, it was birds; now it's cats," he said. He stumbled on the word 'wife,' his face reddened. He kicked the desk with his foot, as though it was something he couldn't get to work.

Layne could not be the only one who noticed his lush lips, his narrow waist that matched his shoulders, and his long clean-shaven neck. There were so many photographs of Mrs. Star in here. Beaming on the walls; posing on his desk; grinning alone; waving as a couple; burnt orange in fall outfits; and mauve in spring ones. No doubt this woman received more gifts than she knew what to do with from her guilty husband.

Where the hell had Layne been looking until now? She was so tired of missing things right in front of her eyes. But she had learned; she would be able to spot a cheating partner in the future. She recalled the secretary going on and on about how Layne had better be on time because Mrs. Star was one of the top criminal lawyers in the city.

Day and night, he dealt with wills and inheritance, far away from the types of people his wife had circulating in her offices. To test a woman like that was not a small decision. This gave her courage. She wanted to be someone it took guts to test, too. A thread wiggled loose.

"My grandmother can relax," Layne said. "And so can you, but we have gone over the count." His eyes were no longer on her. "Sorry about my little dizzy spell there."

Mr. Star's response came out like a grunt. Already he had flung a plaid scarf over his neck, a stray string dangled down his back. His fingers were under her elbow, he steered her to the heavy door, his smile was stretched over his teeth.

"One more thing," Layne said. She wiggled her arm free. "This business with West Dicely." Layne ignored his irritation. He was being paid for his time. "I heard that he was back in town, and might even have reconnected with my brother."

Mr. Star clasped his hands in front of him as if in prayer and bowed his head.

"I'm at your service," he said. His face had folded back to his previous expression. He clicked his tongue against the roof of his mouth as he considered his response.

"I hardly think so."

"Why's that?" Layne's knees trembled and she steadied herself by twirling her bracelet on her wrist.

"West Dicely, the former associate of your brother's, was killed in a car accident a couple of years ago."

"Are you sure?" Layne zeroed in on the lower half of Mr. Star's face, so that his already full lips appeared enlarged.

"People pay me to be sure." The words struck Layne. Was snow falling down her back?

"His grandmother was a client of ours too. We were a much bigger firm then, her direct lawyers have all passed, but I'm old enough to recall her coming in to redistribute things. Besides, it's public knowledge. It was in the locals, nothing I'm sure you would bother keeping up with. Alcohol impairment is a damn shame."

Mr. Star may have said something else, but Layne was no longer listening. In seconds, she rolled through a long ribbon of emotions: anger, humiliation, frustration, relief. The only thing that beat up her brother was Charlie armed with a makeup brush and maybe Baltica, too. Her wildflower nail talents likely extended to the theatrical.

Layne drifted toward the elevator, wishing she had something to dangle from her fingers, the chime of house keys would be so satisfying. She had an old movie ticket in her pocket, and she flicked the rough paper back and forth between her fingers, the hard edge under her thumbnail.

Then, Layne remembered her parents waited for her in the coffee shop. She had skipped the elevator, having no desire to be in a locked, closed space. With a tight chest, she shut her eyes against the squeak as she heaved open the exit door at the bottom of the staircase, and counted each step as she got closer to where they were waiting for her. A voice she liked to think of as her grandmother's, told her not to go, but she could not resist.

Chapter 34

Layne stood outside of the glass coffee shop door looking in. She tried hard to ignore someone's motor revving outside; the fist in her chest; the weakness in her head; the smell of gasoline from the motor revving reminding her of her recent dissociation. Part of her was still sightless in a car speeding to nowhere. Recovery from these episodes could take a while.

They saw her before she saw them and her mother waved from a stool at the coffee bar. More like a raise of the hand, not even a turn at the wrist, or the bend of fingers. Layne was already off the mark; she had been skimming and scanning the tables one by one, saving the bar for last.

The taste of Marvyn's deception was fresh in her mouth, deep in her gums, but it was slowly merging with the tang of her parents' latest reveal. They had tricked Marvyn out of his inheritance, as she had always imagined they would do to her, and still could.

The door swung open. Layne let a couple pass in front of her and in two strides, she was inside the same room as her parents for the first time since she was twenty. Her escape attempt at seventeen fizzled out after six months, when she ran out of savings and options. It took her three more years to slam a door on them for good. Illiana and Pennard swung back and forth on two stools side by side, like restless teens. Layne saw two cups of tap water in front of them, which they sipped while they shuffled their menus between them.

They would get a free meal out of this place, telling the waitress to put it on Mr. Star's account, or some other lawyer in the building directory. They might hint they were here to buy the property, then cry that they had forgotten their wallets in their hotel, and insist they would return when their meeting was rescheduled. If this place was a chain, they could brag about zipping in from provincial central management, or pose as local health inspectors, restaurant reviewers, or employees of a celebrity on the way to shoot a film. So much depended on their moods; the age of the waitress; the presence of a manager; the audience; the weather. This and that, nothing and anything.

They looked bland and professional enough to pull off any number of scams, and knew their lines the way other people knew their timetables or birthdates. These thoughts made Layne feel as though she had weights strapped to her legs. She could vomit if she dwelled on it for too long, but the genetic poison would never come out of her, ever, not if she turned herself inside out, and slept for a week under a power hose.

There was no more space between Layne and her parents. She swayed between their stools with her hands deep in her coat pockets, and kept her emotions as far down in her throat as she could stuff them without using her actual fist.

"Well, young lady. While you have been god-knows-where, your parents have been to hell and back. Are you aware of that?" Illiana said.

"Hell and back," Pennard chimed in.

Layne shifted her weight subtly, a rhythmic movement from one leg to the other, displaying a composed yet restless demeanor. There were no free stools or chairs. It was the height of lunch hour and the place hummed with activity. Her parents spoke to her as if she had been missing for an hour or two, not five years. They did not even pretend to ask how she was or what she had been doing.

"And where's hell these days?" Layne asked. She looked for the waitress who had served her that morning.

"On a cruise?"

"What on earth would we do on a cruise? Especially him." Illiana indicated Pennard with a wave of her head. "Loose as a wet noodle around water. You do remember your father, don't you?"

Illiana ran her hands through her curly hair, then patted Pennard as if he had already lost his lunch over the waves.

Both of them slipped their winter jackets over their stools, flattening them with their behinds. They would never trust their coats to a coat rack; they had ripped off too many coat racks themselves.

"We were over the border, the U.S. stuck in a massive ice storm. Don't they get news in Toronto?"

"Sometimes," Layne said. The truth was, she never read the news after two years of that journalism degree. Consuming more noise was not what she needed, particularly clatter that by definition lasted no longer than the next edition. She got her general information from her students, Virginia's social media pages, and Rael. Neither of her parents was greyer, but she did spot a few more wrinkles around her mother's mouth and forehead, and her father's neck had the sagging skin of an older man.

"Well, we were in the papers. How could you have missed it? You cannot imagine what happened to us. Nobody could have." Her mother pointed at her chest with her thumb.

"Don't ask me how I got the car running." She took a bow, still perched on her stool. Her father clapped.

"I get it," Layne said. "Stuck in the snow?"

"You did hear?" Illiana and Pennard exchanged glances.

"Told you that's why she came," Illiana said to Pennard. Her facial expression exuded satisfaction.

"Thought we wouldn't make it and you would hit the jackpot, eh?"

"Bottom line is, did you sign?" Pennard interrupted his wife.

"It's done."

"Oh my god, payback time," Pennard said. He danced with excitement, swaying his shoulders and wiggling his hips.

"It doesn't bother you that it's Marvyn's, then?" Layne said. "He was framed, remember? Barely out of his teens at the time."

"Are you even listening?" Pennard answered. "Cost us a packet to keep him out of jail. He owes us."

"Marvyn took you cross-border shopping, and the car stalled, he got lost on the way to a gas station."

"It's like you were there. Were you and your brother trying to lose us?" Nausea filtered through her and Layne prayed that was the last of it, that her parents would not say anymore.

"I know you, you knew," Pennard said. He eyed the newspaper like a fat wallet left behind. "Why are you looking at us like that?"

Following her father's eyes, Layne had her answer about the free meal. They did not have to pretend to be celebrities. They had turned a snowstorm into a disaster they were clever enough to survive, an angle they could both work. It was always money, money, money. Settling accounts. They sucked the life out of you. Leeches.

"Wasn't *our* car," Pennard was saying to Illiana. Layne had tuned out. She was very far away. "Let's get that straight."

He flapped the newspaper in his wife's face. Layne jumped back and crashed into a waiter. His full tray of sandwiches, salads and coffees shattered on the floor; splattering hot liquid and salad dressing all over the two of them.

"Oh man," the waiter said. He glared at Layne with such intensity that Layne could not speak.

"I got this, West."

It was the engaged waitress from the last visit, only her ring was gone. Layne was dying to ask her the last name of her boyfriend. West who? She felt confused, grateful, and embarrassed at once. Too many people were staring at her. Her parents' mouths were still moving, but she saw them both in slow motion.

Zigzags of jumbled messes on the floor. Narrow spaces between tables. All of this Layne negotiated before she yanked at the door and only breathed when she got into the air and rested her face on the side of the building, the cold concrete sticking to her lashes. Her head hurt behind her left eyebrow, at the base of her neck, and her feet were not working.

Layne played with the clasp on her bracelet and wanted Rael back, there was no one to keep her mindful anymore, no anchor. Rael loved her. She looked around frantically as if he might appear, but it was Marvyn honking, waving his arms and whistling for her in front of the building as though she were a stray dog.

Marvyn? Another lost thought. Layne had forgotten about him. Jesus Christ. Marvyn had been cheated out of millions of dollars without his knowledge. He had tried to do to her what her parents had already done to him. Layne breathed deeply, but the stench of cigarette smoke made her sneeze. She whirled away from the smell, and forced herself to the end of the curb where the car door was already open for her. She was afraid to look her brother in the eyes; he might read them in an instant and then who could say what he would do?

"Done," she lied, wiping her nose with a tissue she had dug out of her purse. She was careful not to smile, her hand shook as she fumbled with her luggage, she thought about resentment hard, so it would show on her face.

"Airport's waiting." That was not Marvyn's voice. Layne looked up and saw West. Holy shit.

"I thought you ditched me," West said. He pulled out into the street. "But the secretary kept telling me you were there. Good thing."

Where the hell was her brother? She followed West's gaze. She looked over her shoulder and her stomach dropped into her legs. In the backseat, her brother lay unconscious, or worse. She clamped her hand over her mouth, stifling her scream.

Magic Marvyn, always taking the backroad to wherever he wanted, just like Mom and Dad. At least they were smart enough to unblock the tailpipe.

Chapter 35

Layne squeezed her eyes shut. This could not be real. Mr. Star said West Dicely died in a car accident. Then she could have sworn she saw him in that restaurant. She was trapped in so many ways. After traveling so far, her crazy family had her down in the depths, again. She could not tell reality from fantasy; fantasy from her own imagination. Her brother may be dead, or this may be another one of her family's messed-up attempts to gaslight her.

Here she was—desperate for once to be lost in thought, sunk into another world—unable to ignore her physical surroundings. Usually, Layne could dissociate against her will. Now, she was willing and yet her present reality pushed down upon her, choking her air supply. She would do anything not to make eye contact with West, to zap herself out of this passenger seat and onto her flight to Toronto.

The car hummed along and then jerked. She would not look; she would not ask. Do not take the bait, Layne. She repeated this like her last prayer before a code red.

"Layne? Layne?"

He was only saying her name. It meant nothing. It was not a command she had to respond to. She dug her toes into her boots, felt the hard leather through her socks. Layne did not know what was happening, but she was terrified that she might find out.

"Why aren't you dead?"

"What?"

"Someone told me you drank too much and died in a car accident."

"Are the rabble still talking about that? You must mean my uncle West. That's ancient history, but I like the idea you've been talking about me."

"Oh god."

"I used to catch you looking at me, too. Well, you weren't looking for nothing."

The sounds coming out of her own throat sounded animalistic, a combination of pleading and crying. The swerve of the car startled her as it jerked to one side, and she was momentarily preoccupied only with herself. Layne's eyes flew open. She double-checked her seatbelt with one hand and steadied herself on the dashboard with the other.

They were no longer driving, but had jerked to one side. She had to escape. In the backseat, Marvyn was an unnatural shade of blue. Her hands shook. The car smelled like puke.

"Marvyn! Come on." Layne's voice was unrecognizable.

Lightning flashed from nowhere, turning the sky a shiny grey-purple. Layne heard sirens shrieking behind her, beside her, maybe inside of her. There was nothing in her head but more lightning, rain drowned everything around her until nothing was visible through the sheets of water.

"This car is a piece of shit, no way," West shouted. He banged his hand on the steering wheel. "You'll be ruling the roost again soon. We both will."

Layne heard a muffled thud from the backseat. Marvyn's body had shifted, and she caught the faint sound of a moan. Relief washed over her. He was alive.

"Don't pretend to care," West said. "Who are you really worried about? This is a rerun for you."

Layne had no time to lose. She tore her eyes from her brother and grabbed her bag, her heart pounding in her throat. She flung open the door and bolted. In minutes, she was soaked to the bone, panting, her chest heaving. Her hurried steps echoed in the rain-soaked streets, the wet pavement reflecting the dim city lights.

Behind her, West's voice called out, but he was right, the car was a piece of shit, and he could not catch up. Determination to put as much distance between her and West gave her energy, and her eyes scanned the wet world for the yellow light that would signal "airport taxi available."

Chapter 36

VirginiaMakeupartist: Wash-out party. Bed early. GTG

Layne read the message three times. Virginia's immediate response surprised her; she had expected hours of delay. Shifting in the vinyl airport chair next to her departure gate, she was no longer in wet clothes; they now resided in a plastic bag at the bottom of her case, soon to be discarded in the airport bathroom garbage. She had no desire to lay eyes on them again.

Other than a partially swollen lip, Layne looked and felt unchanged, her facade of normalcy intact, her emotional door to her brother closed and sealed. Or so she told herself. Deep down Layne knew Marvyn was in trouble. His theatrics could only go so far. It was too much, even for him. But she refused to acknowledge it. She was done.

Throughout the flight home from Ottawa to Toronto, Layne wrestled with the haunting thought that her brother might be severely injured, maybe permanently. By the time the plane landed, she had convinced herself to let the chips fall where they may. Marvyn had lied to her from the first text, so trying to help him was a waste of time. She chose a compromise between squeezing through the aisle and exiting the plane: she would phone her brother when she was safely in her apartment.

Yet, this resolve wavered as she read Charlie's text message on her phone during her taxi ride home. Charlie's reassurance was conflicting, casting doubt on Layne's determination.

613-375-2037: Listen, I need to tell you something important, but keep it between us. Don't breathe a word to Marvyn. He's fine, so keep cool. And whatever you think you glimpsed, it's not what it seems. We both know how the mind can play tricks. But disappearing like that? It's not responsible. I hoped you'd shown some growth. Mom's been muttering things about you, and I hate to admit she might have a point.

Then, a call from Mr. Star further muddled Layne's emotions. He informed her of a meeting he had arranged with Marvyn to "break the news to him" and urged Layne not to shoulder the burden. The double reassurance, even if it seemed apparent that she did not know the truth, added another layer of uncertainty to Layne's conflicted feelings.

Virginia's text reminding her to pay her bills interrupted her thoughts and shot up her anxiety, which she did not believe possible, pushing her into an emotional danger zone. She clicked on Rael's social media pages and WhatsApp. There were zero posts or updates. Layne refused to acknowledge how winded she was from the last few days, or to let herself imagine her brother's moans all over again. She would not replay her parents' voices either. Desperation to wind back time to the weekend, smothered her, and the best solution was to speak with Rael, but he wasn't there.

When Layne arrived back at her apartment, she bounded up the stairs, her mind swirling with uncertainty about how to approach Rael. All she wanted to do was cry. Instead, she reached into her pocket and pulled out a small stress ball. Squeezing it tightly in her hand, she felt a rush of tension. The sound of the ball squishing echoed faintly in the hallway, a rhythmic beat to accompany her ascent. It felt oddly satisfying, this physical manifestation of her emotions, a silent release after the chaos she had just endured.

"Anyone home?"

Finally inside, Layne was greeted by a chilly silence and a major mess. There were disposable paper plates and cups on every surface. Empty bottles and cans were left uncollected and there was partially eaten food stuck to plates on the dining room table. Almonds, peanuts and loose change adorned the carpets. Hoodies she did not recognize were slung over the backs of chairs and unrecognizable cell phone covers rested on couches.

"Are you trying to make me cry?" she asked the emptiness. "I can't believe it." Blood pounded in her ears. This was all wrong. The apartment was never in such a state. She pushed open a window to air out the smell of incense sticks, scented candles, cigarette smoke, and sweet perfume. She would rather wear a jacket and keep the windows open. Her excitement fizzled to zero. She was certain Virginia would pass on her message to Rael that she was back tonight, maybe earlier. Wasn't she in his arms only yesterday? After four years of dating, how had the gap between them become so wide in so little time? *He only wants you for sport, a pas-sport,* Rael imitating the clerk in Pretoria. Was that what he had said?

A spark of hope lit inside of her as she tossed all of the stained kitchen towels in one heap for the laundry. Maybe Rael was hiding in the bedroom to heighten the romance, or fell asleep waiting for her. He must be warm under the covers, waiting for her to crawl into his arms, so they could begin making up. They did not break up, not for real. It was a fight. He was over it and missed her as much as she missed him.

Now would be all about the two of them because there was nothing to tell. She became manic around her family; that was all— paranoid, extreme, and out of control. She had mourned having a functional family years ago. She would not rub it in that she was right to ignore those text messages. Rael was wrong to think he could understand how her family pushed her to the edge of her very self.

Layne twirled her bracelet and ignored the towels on the floor in the guest bathroom on the way to her bedroom. Empty. She yanked open the closets, peeled back the blankets, threw open the shower curtain in her bathroom; feeling like an idiot, she even peeked under the bed. No one. There was no trace of Rael's belongings. Only the citrusy cologne of his own making hung in the air and made her miss him more. Her heart beat faster. Fear had caught up to her and took over her thoughts, her actions.

She dashed into Virginia's room, which was as much of a disaster zone as the kitchen. Nothing appeared recognizable. The light was on, the sheets were a tangled mess. There was a heap of clothes in the corner. This was so unlike her roommate, but there was no one around to explain. There was the usual fabric softener smell, but the empty laundry rack was tipped over, and the ceiling fan was on full blast in the middle of winter.

Layne put the laundry rack in order and turned off the fan and the light. Her instinct was to text Virginia a flood of questions, but something held her back, like a giant hand on her shoulder. The idea that Rael had already left the country occurred to her. No, he did not change countries like sheets.

Rael must have found a friend of a friend to stay with. He was sulking at his cousin's, the one he disliked, who had taken him to Ottawa in the first place. He needed some space, something she could give him, even though it hurt. She didn't text him. Besides, she might say something about her brother, and that was something she had to bury inside of her. Layne closed the door on Virginia's room and went into her own with wet eyes.

There was no job for her to prepare for, no students to tutor, no boyfriend to be with, no friend to pour her heart out to, and no wedding to plan. Layne stiffened; certain she had left the iron on. She ignored the voice that told her she had not used the iron in four months. She found herself in the laundry room, searching for the iron at the back of the cupboard, unable to stop until she found it, waterless with the plug wrapped around the bottom.

The dryer, then. There was so much fluff in the filter, it was sure to burst into flames, even though it was off. It was only a matter of time, and she might forget about it tomorrow. She yanked open first the dryer door, then the spotless filter, her heart pounding. She zigzagged around the house, sweat at the back of her neck and on her upper lip, examining every plug, pulling on the windows to test the locks, before she double and triple-checked the door lock.

Something was wrong. Danger was everywhere, and it was her job to find it. It lurked somewhere in the universe, something that had taken her brother and could target her too. She never should have taken that step backwards. It had to be undone, all of it. Layne had already deleted every text message, along with her brother's and parents' phone numbers. She had thrown out the clothes she had been wearing in Ottawa and shredded her ticket and boarding pass. What had she forgotten?

Chapter 37

The next day, Layne rode up and down the building elevator in the late afternoon when people who worked trudged and bounced home. She counted neighbors with waxed eyebrows, hair weaves, and false eyelashes as they arrived and departed. As she freed up her ears for the hum of the cables, she felt the rhythm of their rise and fall, exploring the steel framework beneath her fingers.

Underneath the tune of the elevator was one song written by nobody ever: *Trust yourself, let it go, let it go.* When she could no longer hear the melody, when her pulse throbbed in her veins, Layne stepped out of the elevator and counted stairs as she climbed, each step a reminder to trust her instincts. She pushed herself until she was covered in sweat and her heart pounded. Then, she went for a run until exhaustion overtook her.

In the back of Layne's mind, underneath her pain over Rael, part of her was holding her breath for the moment when someone telephoned her about Marvyn. She had to remind herself a thousand times that she had not seen Marvyn, not for years, and had no intention of ever seeing him. Layne had already shredded what she wrote in her diary. Everything.

But there was still the inheritance. She blocked that out too. She had never made a move toward that money, with the exception of signing a few forms. What choice did she have? Anyone would have done the same thing.

Virginia did not answer her phone calls or texts, and never came home. Not Wednesday or Thursday. By Friday, worn out from constant exercising, sleeping alone in the apartment, and disturbed by her roommate's absence, Layne phoned a couple of Virginia's closest friends. They all echoed the same line: she thought it was a hangover, but it turned out she had a bad reaction to antibiotics and went to get some TLC at her sister's place in

Montreal. She would call when she was stronger. She could hardly raise her head off the pillow. Poor thing.

"I bet," Layne murmured into the phone. "Poor thing," she whispered after she had already hung up. There was no sign from Rael either. He had gone cold on social media, and either changed his phone number or was ghosting her. Inside, Layne felt as though the hail storm the other night had wiped out her former life without a trace. She had nothing to follow, no signal in the darkness of uncertainty. Desperate to avoid images of Marvyn turning blue, moaning something she cannot decipher, she struggled to find her footing.

By Saturday night, Layne's claustrophobia was on the verge of engulfing her. She needed to get out, so she asked an Uber driver to take her anywhere he thought would be an entertaining place for a drink, using the pretense she was new in town.

"You should have come in the spring," he said. Then, when she failed to respond: "Why not the Broadboard?"

She had to strain to hear his response and her heart went out to him because the hives on his neck were worse than hers and covered half his face. She tipped him double. The rooftop at the Broadboard Hotel was not a place familiar to Layne. She was not aware of the panorama that comprised both the Toronto skyline and the Don River and had never bothered with local landmarks. But tonight, she imagined something different for herself.

"If it isn't my favorite coquette," a voice behind her said only minutes after her arrival. There was a bounce in the intonation. Someone was excited to see her. "I knew tonight was going to be special."

Layne closed her eyes and wished the voice belonged to someone else. This was so unfair. There were almost three million people in Toronto. Why him?

Still, his presence made her feel more awake and like herself than she had felt all week. This was a familiar role she could play.

"Can I buy you a drink?" Parc plunked himself down on the empty stool next to her. "We could go inside where it's warmer."

"Recycled air isn't for me."

Parc brought a cold breeze with him. She pulled her wrap tighter around her.

"I don't mind. I can smoke out here." He tilted his pack of cigarettes toward her, but she shook her head.

Parc signaled to the waitress and ordered two glasses of white wine. Neither of them spoke for a couple of minutes until the waitress brought their drinks and left. Layne noticed Parc slipped the waitress a hefty tip, and kept his eyes on her ass as she went on to the next customer.

"This is fortunate," Parc said. His voice had changed. She agreed to one drink, and he sounded like wind chimes. "You saved me a phone call. Cheers."

He clinked his glass with hers and they both drank. Layne went nowhere near Parc after-hours, but she didn't work for him anymore. The performance was over; there was no need to stay in the lines. Layne's glass emptied quickly. Parc beamed and rubbed his hands together, blowing on them in the cold. He signaled for two more, with both hands, using each pointer finger.

"You didn't take me up on my offer," he said. "You might like what I have to propose."

"Never been a fan of your offers and proposals," Layne said.

"Things change."

Layne gripped her glass, tempted to throw her drink at him. Instead, she folded her cocktail napkin in half, then in thirds, and quarters. She scratched the back of her neck where itchy hives had been bothering her the last couple of days. If she hung out too long with Parc, they would expand into welts.

There were seven other people outside with them. Four men and three women. Only one woman was in a dress. The music was acapella and on low, it was still early, not yet hardcore party time.

With less than a dozen people outside, the noise was a low hum, as she liked it.

"There are two things I need to tell you, Layney," Parc said, forcing her attention away from the music. He slipped a hard candy into his mouth and moved it from side to side with his tongue.

Layne was too exhausted to demand he close his mouth while he sucked. It was enough that she had to listen to him. Nothing he could reveal would make a difference. Her heart was broken, she was in a relationship wasteland, and she did it to herself. Who would want to marry into a family like hers, which was even worse than she thought it was? Rael must have sensed his chance, and she was the one who gave it to him.

"One is business, the other is, let us say, social. Which one do you want to hear first?" Layne gave him a look, which he ignored.

"Come on," he said. "Order is your game."

The comment undressed her. What else had Parc gleaned about her? She leaned on the bar, downed her second drink, and held up one finger. She liked her numbers in order.

"Number one it is. We are using this hybrid business to our advantage and opening up another branch in Hamilton."

"Congratulations," she said. She sucked on the piece of lemon that decorated her glass. The sour taste was satisfying. She did not care how it looked to Parc. Let him think she was trying to seduce him using his own methods.

"There's no reason for one slip to eclipse two years of hard work."

"There was no slip. He fell."

"Of course." Layne glared at Parc, but his nose was in a menu.

"I'm peckish," he said, fanning the menu. There was no way she was eating a meal with Parc.

"You're schlepping this out on purpose."

"I suggested you head the new team. Ta dum!" Parc opened his arms wide, palms open and up, as though he had made their drinks disappear. She pictured him then pursing his lips, ready for his thank-you kiss right away. They were thin, puckered, moist, and coming closer. Her glass was empty. The room spun.

"Forget it," Layne said, snapping out of it.

The last thing she needed was a new partnership with Parc. Or was it? The dimly lit bar buzzed with activity, the air heavy with the scent of alcohol and the murmur of conversations. The waitress who had caught Parc's eye before winked at him and blew him a kiss. The moment passed. Layne forced herself to look at Parc with new eyes. He was staring at her breasts, his mouth slightly open as he drank. If she was careful and didn't make any mistakes, Parc's new offer could be her escape route, a reward, a way to go forward.

Chapter 38

Layne excused herself and went to the bathroom where she washed her hands, applied more anti-itch cream to her neck, rubbed it in trying not to make the skin redder, and skipped reapplying lipstick. She took her time brushing her hair, threw a few odds and ends out of her purse, and rinsed her mouth.

Finally, she could not take the stale bathroom air anymore. She was pleased to see Parc was still there, waiting for her. He wanted her badly, but she had to make sure he wanted her blindly.

"Rinata's way ahead of me in experience and she has finished her master's. Why wouldn't the director go for that?" she asked.

She was always careful not to say James. She could not risk giving anything away. Layne stood so that she was eye level with Parc as he sat.

"About that," Parc said. He unbuttoned the top two buttons of his shirt. "The director's taken leave of a sort and I'm his replacement."

"Is that so?" Layne said. She thought of Virginia stood up at her party. "Well, here's to progress."

"What do you say?" Parc asked.

"About what?"

He eyeballed her. "God you're a tease. Hot cold. Cold hot. You know it's irresistible, right?"

Layne liked his answer for once. She wanted him to feel her eyes on him as she stared at his crotch. "Your mind's working, nice promotion, nice raise, great look on your resume."

"Is this a trick?"

"There's a cure for those goosebumps." He held out his jacket.

Layne was cold and had been so eager to get out of her house before she changed her mind, that she had forgotten her coat and her wrap was thin. Layne let Parc put his blazer around her, it was still filled with his body heat and sweat. Another drink and this would be a lot easier to pull off. A cocktail appeared on the table.

Parc encouraged her. "It's called Cheaper Than Therapy. Vodka-based." He tilted his head toward the drink and sucked on jellybeans one by one. Maybe there was a dish of them on the bar he'd cleaned out. She stuck her hand in the side pocket of his blazer. Hard candies, jellybeans, and a lollypop. She could not hold back, burst out laughing and his eyes lit up.

"Say you'll think about it," Parc said. "I'll email you the formal details. You would be perfect. You are perfect, Layney."

Layne looked into his eyes. He wanted her to feel special, like the center of attention, but for how long? He was the type who blows away with the slightest breeze. This ruminating would kill her. She knew precisely who Parc was.

"Is this a trick, Parc? Does this new location exist?" She chewed on the end of her straw, tasting her own lipstick.

"This location is perfect. Are you paying attention to the view?"

"I'm asking a question," Layne said.

He laughed. "Time for number two." Parc's blazer fell off Layne's shoulders and onto the floor, she shook her head when he offered it to her again, and hung it over his arm.

She could see sweat above Parc's upper lip. They were both warm from the alcohol. The wind blew Layne's hair across her face and she let it. It stuck in her earring. She fixed her hair and arranged herself on the stool so that her knees faced Parc and twirled her ice cubes around in the glass. Two had already melted. There were four left.

"I'm only the messenger," Parc said.

"Is that your new title these days?"

Parc's hand brushed Layne's shoulder. The terrace got a lot brighter. Waitresses were setting up outdoor heaters.

"Would you like to move to a table?" the bartender asked them. "Entertainment's starting." He waved over a waitress and whistled, pointed at Layne and Parc. Layne followed behind the waitress, who guided her to a table next to a blazing heater. She yawned and cracked her knuckles in one hand. Snap, snap, snap.

"A picture's worth a thousand words, but what's the value of a recording?" Parc stuck his hand into his back pocket and took out his cell phone. He scrolled through it, and when he found what he was looking for, he put the phone on the table. With his eyebrows, he gestured for her to pick up his phone.

Layne leaned forward, hesitated, grasped Parc's phone and looked at the screen. It took a few seconds for her eyes to focus in the dim light. She pressed play. The background noise was loud in her apartment, the usual trance music and hum of conversation.

You're right into it. Virginia's drunk voice, her French-Canadian so strong it was hard to tell she was speaking English.

Another cup? Rael's voice. His twisty accent bursting through as it always did when he was drunk, all his a's sounding like i's, his c's hard like k's (*Inother kup?*), as though he'd never left Johannesburg.

I have more for both of us. It's a lot quieter in my bedroom. Want to lie down? Not alone. Who said anything about being alone?

The recording ended and it was nothing to picture Virginia taking Rael's hand, and both of them getting lost in the crowd on their way to Virginia's bedroom. Nobody said anything for a minute. There was a heat spreading through Layne's chest.

"That potion maker was never for you," Parc said, finally. He put his head close to Layne's speaking in her ear. "Traipsing around the globe like students, roommates at your age, nothing but virtual communication for ages. Who studies herbs? You're way above that. You deserve so much more. You're—"

"Shut up." Layne put her hands over her ears and pushed back her hair. "Why were you recording?"

"For you." He pulled his chair in and leaned forward. "I noticed your guy on his own gravitating toward your roommate. I look out for your interests."

"You crashed the party for my interests?"

"Yes, the promotion. I figured you would be back."

A roar from the customers. Some local celebrity made an entrance. A vlogger or a YouTuber. People clapped, cheered, the seven customers had morphed into a crowd. Tables were dragged out of the way to create a dance floor. The volume was turned up on the music, something seductive and old, Beyoncé's "Blow."

It was easy to believe the intimate words were aimed right at the listener. She could not look Parc in the eye with this song playing, the silky voice that made its way onto your own tongue, turned you on.

"We're both strangers here in this city." Parc went on. "We have to protect one another. You will thank me eventually. I have loads of patience. Come on, get that look off your face. Surprised? We don't need either of them. I would not look back if I were you. The universe has done you a favor."

The music went on about humming and moaning, humming and moaning. Parc could not resist. He left her alone at the table with the recording while he clapped and swayed and bumped with the waitress, who was now off duty and circling Parc, shimmying low to reveal the tops of her breasts, no doubt remembering his heavy tip that for Parc was now paying off.

Chapter 39

When Layne heard the creak of the door, she held her body rigid, kept her eyes on the screen. She continued to watch television on the couch where she had been all day. It was Sunday, so she did not have to feel like an outcast in her sweatpants and a hoodie, doing nothing but flicking through Netflix.

Layne did everything to squirm away from those pictures in her mind, which Parc had painted for her with his recording. Virginia naked from the waist up with her pants undone, kissing Rael on the mouth. Both of them undressed lying side by side on the bed. Layne wished she could press the button on her imagination. She was certain Parc made several copies of his recording as an insurance policy.

Her mind skipped back to the recording. Virginia and Rael. Rael and Virginia. The recording. Drunk and pissed off, rejected, hurt and alone in Virginia's bedroom. Her thoughts merged with the images in her mind until she never wanted to speak to either of them again.

"I'm back," Virginia said. The lock of the door. The scraping of a suitcase. "Was really out of it there for a while, but my sister's the best. Still not fully charged, but have to organize for work tomorrow." Virginia blabbed on. How the antibiotics were the wrong prescription, the idiot doctor, the idiot pharmacist, the superwoman sister.

"Look what I brought you." There was a bouquet of white and yellow lilies in Virginia's hand. "Well, brought us, you know, to urge spring to get here already."

Virginia hung up her leather jacket, slid out of her high heeled boots, and pulled her gloves off from the wrist, rolled them together like pairing socks. Her chin- length dirty blonde hair shone and matched her skin. She did not look like she was recovering from anything more than a five-and-a-half-hour Sunday drive from Montreal.

"I was hoping you would be over it, but I get why you're angry." Layne flicked off the television and eyed Virginia. "I left the place a hot mess. I'm sorry. Je suis désolé. You did not deserve that. Thanks for the cleaning and I'll make it up to you. We'll go out for an expensive dinner, eh?"

Virginia dragged her suitcase in from the front door. She strode into her room and Layne could hear her opening and closing cupboards and drawers. She flipped stations without seeing anything, jealousy burning a hole in her stomach.

"Had your usual yogurt? I brought tons of goodies from my mom's house." Virginia was in the kitchen now, taking stock of the fridge, the pantry, the cupboards.

"Off dairy," Layne answered.

"Oh, come on. I said I was sorry. It was a long time ago now. Coffee? No, I'm not 100 percent better yet. Let's have tea."

The kettle rumbled. A cupboard opens, mugs hit the counter. She waited until Virginia returned to the living room with two hot teas, tapping her foot on the carpet, twirling her hair with her pointer finger behind her ear.

Then Layne burst. "I never heard from Rael. You know, my boyfriend?" Layne tripped over his name; it had become a foreign word.

"Are you asking me something?" Virginia blew on her tea.

"Am I?" Layne wished her roommate would blush, stammer, something, but she did not even miss a beat.

"The truth is I brought all of this food for us, but also for James," Virginia said.

"I don't care about your food." Layne grabbed her tea, stood, sauntered to the sink, and dumped the hot liquid down the drain. She slammed the cup on the counter.

"I told him to come by, but dinner will just be the two of us," Virginia continued as though Layne had not moved or spoken. "Don't worry."

"No one's worried about you," Layne said. She swayed back and forth. Her stomach so far down her body.

"I'll meet him after for drinks. I'm over it, his no-show at the party." Virginia sipped her tea and wiped her mouth with the back of her hand. "Or I think I am."

"I'm not your therapist."

"We need to talk it out, his sudden disappearances are getting longer. That's not in our agreement. Couples have agreements, you know?" Virginia's eyes met Layne's.

"Can't say that I do," Layne said. She wished she could tower over Virginia, but of course, her roommate was a head taller than her. "Have you heard from Rael?"

"He will not be able to resist me; I got a new leather skirt, a silk top. Both wow."

As far as she knew, James was on leave from Parc, but Layne kept that to herself. She refrained from mixing work with any other part of her life, mindful that divulging such information could potentially backfire. Perhaps his actual wife had a baby, and he was on paternity leave, or maybe he had another girlfriend.

It wasn't worth the risk while she was still considering Parc's job offer, though deep down she knew that changing her location would bring relief. She shook her head to clear it. She had to stop thinking like Virginia's girlfriend. This woman had invited her boyfriend into her bedroom.

Eyeing Virginia as she moved around the kitchen carefree, guilt-free, humming as she poured more tea, added, stirred, tasted, poured—all of it made Layne's brain fog.

"You can stop pretending. And don't worry about making it up to me. I'm moving out." Layne kept her gaze steady. They were both in the living room again now. They had been circling each other since Virginia came home.

"Pretending? What did you say?" Virginia sipped her tea and leaned back on the couch. Up close, Layne could see the bags under her eyes. Maybe she was sick from antibiotics or guilt.

"You slept with Rael, don't deny it."

There was a long silence and it weighed on Layne so heavily, she had to stand, pace the room, try to throw it off.

"I'm sorry," Virginia said. She spoke slowly like a robotic recorded message. "I must have heard wrong."

"I didn't say it wrong," Layne said.

"What did he tell you?" Virginia asked.

"Nothing. Like I said, I haven't heard from him."

"So where are you getting this bullshit from?"

"What does it matter? I know."

Virginia clasped her fingers together. She rubbed her eyes, smearing mascara all over her fists. "This would look different over a nice dinner, but have it your way," Virginia said. "It was a party. This old-fashioned display is pathetic, really."

"Do you mean a private party?"

"It was nothing."

"Don't touch me," Layne said, backing away from Virginia's hug.

"I understand you threw him out. Were you thinking he wouldn't need comfort after that?"

The neighbor's phone rang and rang. Dogs barked in the hallway. It wasn't enough for Layne. She wanted Virginia's voice drowned out. For once, she prayed no one would pick up, that the dogs would become more frantic for a door to open.

"He's a real man, Layne, not something out of your fantasy-prone personality"

"Shut up," Layne screamed.

"After all the trouble he went to, surprising you. The expensive jewelry. You're a brat. What were you expecting?"

"Too much apparently."

Virginia's nostrils flared. She got in Layne's face.

"It's pathetic that you picked a fight with your boyfriend, Layne, and now you're blaming me."

"You weren't even there," Layne said.

"Take responsibility for your actions."

"Even if I screwed up with Rael, say that I did. That means you can jump into bed with him?"

"I can assure you it was the other way around."

Layne picked up the mug of tea and threw it at the wall where it shattered to pieces. The second mug followed suit, then a book, a vase, a phone, anything she could get her hands on. The dogs outside barked incessantly at the front door, while the neighbor's phone alternated between silence and persistent ringing.

"You can clean that up after I spent hours putting this place back together, and by the way, don't ever speak to me again."

Layne only heard Virginia in the background of her mind, if she said anything at all. She had already left the room to pack. Then, she would text Parc and tell him she was accepting his offer. It was no longer possible to think straight in this city; she had to get out of here.

Chapter 40

Music, that's what Layne needed. To unwind and let her thoughts flow on their own. Through the curtains, high beams lit up her living room. The garbagemen outside rolled the squeaking cans into the truck. A car alarm whirred. What was going on at this hour in this unfamiliar city?

Nothing was obvious to her in Hamilton; a port city of half a million, 58 kilometers southwest of Toronto. So much was coming out of nowhere. So many things arrived to her from the unknown. Too many items to absorb at once.

Layne opened her phone and pressed a music app and the first playlist without looking, then she pressed it up to full volume. A knock at the door, and she did not have to work hard to feel annoyed.

"Wrong address," she shouted. It must be another delivery person. She had come to the conclusion that she was the only one of her new neighbors who still went to actual stores. There was none of the coming-and-going and mingling of her apartment building in Toronto.

Here, everyone kept to themselves and interacted with delivery people only, the doors opened no more than a crack. Her reception was weak and the volume on her phone was faltering, she strained to tune into the music. The knocking continued.

"Must be for someone else," she shouted louder. Layne did not want to buy anything, had no extra almond milk or coconut sugar, and could not help anyone lost; she barely knew her way around. She had to get back to her one-woman secretary/manager/curriculum developer and admissions officer job. If only she could just have an hour to clear her buzzing mind. The phone hummed.

Rael: Planning to ignore me all night?

Stunned, she dropped her phone. She changed her number the day after she returned from Ottawa, so there was no way it could be him.

"Great," she said. "Now it's broken."

She bent to retrieve her phone and read the newly-cracked screen. 'Block' or 'accept contact'?

Layne Fortunefield: Who is this?
Rael: Open the door and find out.

Layne peered through the keyhole. Rael was holding a candy bouquet in one hand and a bunch of red roses in the other. An unsettled feeling rose inside of her. How could that be Rael? She must be dreaming. She rushed to the freezer and stuffed a handful of ice in her mouth. Then, she dried her chin and neck with a towel, knocking over the dish soap and the cutlery holder in the process. The soap bottle cracked and leaked onto the floor tiles. Handfuls of knives, spoons and forks clattered into a dirty pot Layne had left soaking.

In the hall mirror, she saw someone miserable with something stuck between her teeth. The knocking began again. Seventeen bangs on the door.

"Please, Layne," he shouted with conviction in his voice. "It's cold."

Yoga pants and a sweatshirt. Too relaxed. In her bedroom, she flossed her teeth, changed into a beige skirt with an off-white blouse. She oiled her hair so it was silky not frizzy, and wiped the leftover oil on a towel.

"I'm not going away," Rael said. "You're not even letting me talk to you. Isolating yourself won't work. I'm not your brother, I'm not your parents, and I'm not giving up."

Her stomach clenched at the word 'brother' and before she knew it, tears cascaded out of her eyes. She knew she was crying for herself. The wave of emotion started in the pit of her stomach and moved up her chest, into her throat and poured out her mouth. Pressure wouldn't work. Bang, bang, bang.

"What are you doing here? How did you find me?" she yelled at the door. "Think I'm sitting around waiting for you?"

"Let me in and I'll tell you everything you want to know," Rael said.

"Why should I?" Layne asked.

"Because you want to." There was a pause. "And because I love you."

Layne felt a pain in her heart that made her knees tremble. His words warmed her lips. Because you want to. But it was fake, all of it.

"You get two minutes," she said. Layne flung the door open, her heart beating in her throat. She made a show of looking at her watch, a gift for their first-year anniversary.

"Does my two minutes start when I'm inside all the way?" he said.

As she stepped back, Rael entered the room, and she released a breath she hadn't realized she'd been holding.

"For you," he said, indicating the flowers and the candy. "Please."

Careful not to touch his fingers, Layne took the bouquet and padded the twelve steps to the kitchen. An empty water bottle was all she had for a vase. She cut off the top with scissors, arranged the flowers, and placed the vase on the only table in the apartment. The candy she left on the counter.

"I wanted to see how you were," he said.

She shook her head and squeezed her eyes shut. She wished she could control her feelings, she wanted to hate him. Hate him, hate him. His hands had been on Virginia; his soft mouth, his tanned skin. She perched on the edge of the couch, arms crossed at her chest, one leg gracefully swung over the other.

"Wasn't easy to find you. That boss of yours your personal bodyguard or something?"

Layne glared at Rael. She scratched her throat and pulled her collar as high as it could go over her neck. "One more minute," she said.

"I'm sorry I wasn't there when you got back, then I went cold. I needed to think. Then, when I went to your apartment, Virginia told me you had moved. Took me a while to find you. I went to your work, and that idiot wouldn't tell me anything. I was a jerk for not calling." The sting hurt.

"Yes, you were."

"You were not perfect either."

"I did not sleep with your best friend!" She ran her hands through her hair. "And don't bother telling me how drunk you were."

"This is such a waste of time."

"Cheat! Liar!" she said. She had to keep her breathing under control. She had to stay in her body.

"Look, you're not taking this seriously, are you? Virginia and I are not a thing. It was nothing. I thought you were more modern."

"More modern?"

"Actually, yes."

"I'm the problem? How many others have there been? Are each of your soaps inspired by one of them?"

Layne opened her phone and pressed play on the recording, but she could not listen to it again and went outside on the balcony, leaving Rael to listen alone. Outside, she breathed in the cold air and tried to care that it was such a pretty winter night, full of shining stars against a black sheet of sky.

Instead, she picked up one of the white plastic chairs on the balcony, scanned for any passerby in the empty field below that was often used as a hangout for teenagers, and tossed it over the edge. She waited for the crash as it hit the ground behind the building.

The bang felt good. Parc brought over the two chairs as a housewarming gift. They looked like the types of chairs that belong in a school cafeteria and depressed Layne every time she glanced at them. They had to go.

Chapter 41

"Hey, I'm not next, am I?" Rael asked, but it was too late. The sharp leg of a chair cut into his cheek before he could stop it. She raised it into the air again. Breathing deeply, he held her arm in mid-throw, the chair dangling above their heads. Gently, he took the chair out of her hand.

"I thought you had these physical outbursts under control," Rael said.

"You are talking to me about control," she answered. "How about control with my roommate, who was supposed to be my friend." Layne grabbed the chair and hurled it over the edge before Rael could stop her, then ran back inside, slamming the balcony door.

"I'm bleeding, are you happy? Can we speak like adults?"

"Hopefully, you'll leave," Layne said.

"I'll leave if you want me to, but let me finish." Rael banged the bathroom door closed, and Layne could hear him cleaning himself up. "It was just the dumbest thing I've ever done," he said when he came out. "All it did was make me realize how much I missed you. You're dreaming up the wildest things in your head. I know you. Stop. It's so destructive."

"Destructive?" Layne said.

Rael scooped Layne into his arms and she let him. She felt as she always did when he held her, as though he must have held her in all of her past lives, she was so at home next to him.

"I want to go back to where we were until we were so terribly interrupted and my elaborate surprise was ruined. Remember?" Rael whispered in her ear.

Layne wished she could forget. The warmth from his lips on her ear traveled beyond her fingers and toes into the air. He angled her chin so she was looking into his eyes, red with fatigue.

"It wasn't so long ago," Rael said. "I never should have separated the engagement bracelet from the rest of the set. And leaving you alone in Ottawa was a mistake, too. You were so wound up. I should have waited until you calmed down. Those couple's therapy sessions seemed so easy. I was sure I could do this with you, and I failed the first test."

Rael brushed his fingers against hers and Layne lit up inside even warmer than she was already. She smelled his familiar scent and felt a little dizzy. How she missed him. There might as well have been a rope tying them together. He kissed Layne for so long that she felt as though she would never have to deal with her real life again.

The sound of the music she was playing was in her ears and her emotions were tangling in one tight knot in her throat. Rael stopped kissing Layne, slipped his hand into his pocket, and pulled out a velvet box. He opened it and removed a thin white gold band with a round diamond in the middle and two small round diamonds on either side. He did not need to say anything. Every moment away from him was agony.

Pushing Rael away was like a hook in Layne's heart. He dropped the ring and it bounced on the ground and she lost sight of it. He scrambled to find it.

"The thing is that we can't go back to where we were, Rael."

"Why not? People fight. People make mistakes. People move on."

He held the ring in one hand, the velvet box in the other. It was a perfect match to her bracelet, only she wasn't wearing it. The bracelet was buried at the bottom of her top drawer in her room.

"It's the images. I can't get those images of you in bed with Virginia out of my head."

"Oh my god. Yes, you can. I hardly remember them myself."

Layne covered her face with her hands, not wanting Rael to see into her anymore. She took the ring out of Rael's hand, afraid to touch it for too long. It belonged to someone else. She opened the box, replaced the ring and handed it back to him.

"Please go. Please just go."

Layne returned to the balcony, but left the door open this time and held her breath until she heard the front door open and close. She saw the broken white plastic chairs only one floor down, shattered in the field. There was enough street light to see she had cracked them both.

Chapter 42

Guilt nagged Layne about Rinata, the senior teacher at the language institute, the one who should be in charge of opening the new branch. She felt complicit in Parc's harassment, taking this job from her. The promotion should have gone to the person with more qualifications, more experience and education, not the person Parc wanted to get into bed.

But Parc could get a lot of women into bed. He had an obsession with Layne and she knew it. He thought they mirrored each other in ways that they didn't. Part of her even liked it, maybe encouraged it. She did not know anymore.

Layne's head spun as she considered how easily she bought Parc's story about the Hamilton branch. She could not recall if she had eaten or drunk that day. Too much of her energy was going into blotting out the image of her brother bruised and moaning, no matter how she tried to edit it. She received a crazy text out of the blue after five years and deleted it, that's what really happened.

Layne hadn't heard one word about this new branch from the director, who was on some undefined break, or from anybody else for that matter. No one on staff had emailed her a letter of congratulations, support, or encouragement, so it wasn't real. Yet, she had an office, a whole floor of empty classrooms, computers and a budget.

A pain above her left eyebrow sharpened and Layne slowed down. She needed a break before the long drive back to Hamilton. Now she remembered. The last thing she had eaten was yesterday's dinner, a bag of frozen broccoli smothered in parmesan cheese. Parc was keeping her so busy setting up this school, that she forgot to eat. Layne pulled over at the first café and stamped her feet at the entrance, trying to get her blood to circulate after so much sitting. It came to her that she was about to phone Virginia and then Rael. That was the real reason she stopped in here. Those were the only two people who could settle her. She needed closure. Hate wasn't helping her move forward. But what would she say? The right phrases would come to her, or she would stumble over the wrong ones and rearrange them until they came out right.

A large hot chocolate with marshmallows and a whole chocolate cake. Layne would eat as much as she wanted and take the rest home and freeze it. Her empty freezer was depressing. Virginia had always kept their freezer full of her mother's pea soup and Shepherd's pies.

After staring into space for ten minutes, Layne interrupted the only employee she could see, who was reluctant to get off the phone. The place was empty except for a group of teenagers in a booth making TikTok videos and falling all over themselves with laughter. She watched them until one girl stuck her tongue out at her and motioned for her to stop staring at her boyfriend. She reddened and sucked on each marshmallow one by one until there was nothing left but hot chocolate. She drank and started on the frosting layer of the cake. After three bites, it was time to get the pressure off her chest and call Virginia.

Layne held her breath while the phone rang, once, twice, three times.

"Allo?" Virginia said.

"It's me."

"I have caller ID. You still owe for utilities, that's why I answered."

Layne swallowed. She rolled the empty hot chocolate cup back and forth on the table.

"I'm calling to say I should have settled my bills before I left." Layne was inventing this; she hadn't given a second thought to outstanding accounts. She wanted Virginia to apologize and she hated herself for wanting it.

"Oh, I've added the charge for the broken cups. Acting like a two-year old has a price," Virginia said.

Layne reddened. She was such an idiot. She deserved an award for the world's dumbest person. She had no one to blame but herself for picking up the phone. Virginia would never back down.

"Just text me the total."

"I did a lot for you. Covered for you more than once on rent, tried to introduce you to people. You're the one who threw out your boyfriend. I've been supportive of you in many ways, even when it got complicated."

"I missed the complicated part."

"Everything has to be spelled out for you, even now. You're obsessed with detail."

"Look, I'm not saying you weren't a good friend once but after what's happened," Layne began. "You realize that?" Layne sat straighter. She was unsure how she came to be in the defensive position.

The teenagers flashed their phones on her and she realized she was about to be in the background of a TikTok video. She dashed to another table, juggling her phone and the cake.

"I'm willing to talk about this in person," Layne said. "I'd really like to know more specifically what happened."

Virginia's laugh was heartless. "Why?"

"It matters to me," Layne answered.

"I'll tell you what matters. Rael is only the beginning. You think I'm a sucker, dating an older man?"

"This was never about you."

"You're no less a sucker, Layne. You're the same as me, another woman men run circles around until you're so dizzy, they lead you by the nose."

"What's that supposed to mean?"

"Enjoying your fake promotion?" Virginia said. She laughed so loud Layne had to move the receiver away from her ear. "I hear you're all heated up about it."

"Fake promotion?" Layne said. Her fingers gripped the phone. The dancing, gyrating, lip-syncing teenagers were getting louder, closer, too close.

"Parc wasn't authorized to go ahead with this idea on his own," Virginia said. "He took advantage of his temporary status filling in for my boyfriend on leave to give you something that's not yours. I guess he figures by the time the real boss gets back, you'll already be in his bed, if you're not calling from there already. Wake up, Layne. You're doing all the groundwork for someone else until you're flat on your back. Or is it too late?"

Virginia hung up.

Layne stabbed the chocolate cake until there was nothing left but a huge creamy mess. She continued raking the cake with a fork until it was mush.

"Miss Fortunefield?" Layne jerked her head and saw Marco staring from her to the cake. He held a spray bottle and a rag, and his t-shirt had a tag with his name pinned over the left side of his chest.

"Do you work everywhere?" she asked. She moved the demolished cake to the end of the table.

"I work every chance I get."

"I remember."

"Mind if I sit?" he asked. Layne shrugged her shoulders. Adrenalin pumped through her, but she preferred avoidance mode. She wouldn't think about her conversation with Virginia in public. Not here, not now, not in front of Marco.

"I want you to know I'm sorry," Marco said. "I was told he'd pass me without coming to any more classes if I let him do whatever he wanted with those photos and videos and that freed me up to work. I've had bad luck ever since. I lost my nursing job, my car broke down, my dog got sick. But I prayed for a sign and well, here you are. You're it."

"I'm a sign?" Layne asked.

"Yes. Things will turn around if I confess. I was waiting for something to happen. I'm sending a recording now, as soon as you leave."

Layne held up her hand in a stop motion, the weight of his words was too much for her to handle.

"Who?" she said.

"Excuse me?"

"Who told you he'd pass you?"

Marco stared at his lap.

"Parc?" Layne said.

Marco nodded while he cleaned her table, gathered the crumbs into his palm and threw them away. "Let's not talk names. I don't want any more bad luck and anyone could be listening."

"I understand and I forgive you."

"You still want the cake?" He smiled at her. "I can carry it to your car. Change your mind about a party?"

"I don't think that's a cake anymore and there's no need for another," Layne said. She had an idea. She would invite Parc to the date of his life, dinner for two alone in the office. There was no time to lose. She stood and held her hand out to Marco, who shook it. "A whole cake is too big for a little goodbye party."

"I was right. You are making a party?"

"I guess you could say that. A very private one. Just me and one other person."

In the parking lot, her hand froze in her pocket with the car keys. She remembered her peppermint oil and yanked it out of her purse, sprayed it on her wrists and took deep breaths until she could drive. There was no reason to go back on her plan, the one she had come up with at that bar in Toronto. Virginia's laugh still echoed in her head. Marco's apology. Her mind was hurling through time and space while she stood in a half-empty parking lot, dangling her keys.

"Miss Fortunefield," Marco called from the café entrance. He was holding two paper bags. "From me. Some rolls and cookies. For your private party. Please take it all."

Layne shook her head, no. She didn't want any rolls or cookies, or anything else.

Chapter 43

Parc scooped another pile of caramelized onions onto his plate. "You sure you don't want some?" he asked. "They're delicious."

Layne shook her head. "Got plenty," she said, though there were none on her plate.

Only ten minutes ago, she was working alone in the new college, answering potential student emails, and reviewing teacher resumes. The college was spacious and airy, but the oversized furniture made her feel cramped. Plus, she hadn't assembled the bookcases due to a lack of time. Then, she realized there was no need to economize, so she ordered new furniture and scheduled someone to deal with the bookcases.

It was her second week here and today she added a couple of ferns she prayed she would not drown and real silk panel curtains. She had always hated the no pictures, no plants, no curtains atmosphere in the Toronto college that took bland to a new level. The whole place was blue carpets and white walls. Her college would have some flair with beanbag chairs and a kitchen with a coffee machine, free soft drinks and fresh pastries with no-sugar and gluten-free options.

Parc breezed in, setting off the wind chimes Layne hung over the front door. His arms were burdened with boxes of takeout piled so high; she could not see his face. He insisted she take a break and have lunch with him, even though it was four o'clock in the afternoon.

"These have bits of cheddar cheese on them. Your favorite." He pointed to mini triangular pieces of toasted pita, which he'd brought with an accompanying fig sauce. She prayed he wouldn't tell her figs were erotic because of their scent and texture again. His approach was growing stale.

"I thought it was vegan," she said.

"Just the cheese pops. The side dishes are from a Middle Eastern place. That one's cauliflower with sesame sauce. Don't tell me you don't love that. And this fried eggplant is out of this world."

Layne didn't ask Parc where he got his ideas about her taste buds. Parc had been that way since she met him, he intuited things about her she had never revealed, another creepy element to his personality. But his way of relating to her had become familiar, she expected this established part of their banter, even if she didn't care to admit it, like his flirting. Meanwhile, he had blackmailed a student as well as given her a promotion only to get her into bed.

"Aren't you hungry?"

Before Layne could answer, Parc scooped a tablespoon of crumbed cauliflower dripping in sesame sauce on her plate. "Oh dear," he said. The serving spoon came too close to her chest and now she had sesame sauce dripping down her taupe blouse onto her black skirt. "How clumsy, my apologies."

He dug in the takeout bag for a napkin and wiped the front of her blouse, before she could dart out of the way.

Layne scowled at him and excused herself. She did her best in the bathroom mopping up the mess with water, but now the front of her blouse was wet and the lines of her bra showed through. She slipped on her winter jacket; there was no way she would eat in a wet shirt with Parc.

"Are you going to be comfortable in that heavy thing?" he asked, when she returned to their meal.

"Food's not calling to me," Layne answered.

He frowned at her and impatience showed on his face. Layne reread the text message from Mr. Star. The one where he wrote she could count on him twice, how he did not have a bias toward her parents, and that she would not end up like her brother. Layne was too scared to ask if that meant double-crossed, beaten up, or missing. She plucked vegan cheese pop onto a napkin and nibbled at it, perched on the corner of her desk. She was careful not to sit in a way that allowed Parc to see up her skirt.

Outside, an ambulance siren warned drivers to pull off to the side of the road. Busses rumbled down the street, reminding Layne to add bus routes to the new website. The college was in a great location for students without cars.

"Remember that recording?" she asked. Her hand covered half her face. It was hard to get the words out and the food down.

"Recording?" Parc bowed his head close to his plate.

"The one from the party at my old apartment."

Parc finished another mouthful of eggplant. He twirled his glass around on the table. "You don't have to thank me."

Layne stared at her hands. Parc could still blow her away with how his mind worked.

"It's hard to move on, isn't it? I bet you thought you could not do it, but here we are. I left London alone, came here with nothing. We have so much in common."

She responded dryly, "Do we? Because leaving a city and arriving with nothing might be where our similarities end."

"Not at all. We both have to be self-reliant, don't we? It's obvious to anyone who knows how to look that we are made of the same stuff. I see how you react when people ask you about your parents and I get it. Mine kept things from me they had no right to keep."

Layne shifted in her chair, jiggling her leg over one knee. If he had picked up on her tone of voice, it didn't show. It was so easy to stir-up the conversation, change the margins. But her mind blanked and Parc was settled in.

"My mother loved to cook and bake, all of my school meals were homemade. Anglican school, you know, Church of England. The boys used to see my lunches, the foreign smells and spices and laugh at me, toss my lunch around like I was a chimp in the middle. I would come home on weekends too ashamed to say anything." Parc stared off over Layne's shoulder. "My father was from Manchester, but my mother wasn't British. She lives in Madrid now."

"You're Spanish?" Layne said. "I never realized you could speak to the students because it was a language you learned at home. Figured you took a few classes."

"Hardly," Parc answered. "The point is, I'm not like everyone else. And I've learned to get by on my own, like you."

"Do you think this is getting by?" Layne asked.

"You're right." He brought his fingers together and kissed them. "We more than get by. We kill it, the two of us. We belong together." He pointed at the pile of zucchini sticks and stabbed one with his fork, ignoring her question. "You must try these while they're hot."

Parc forked the biggest zucchini stick onto her plate and cut it into pieces the size of croutons and then into pieces the size of soup nuts. He pushed the plate closer to her. It rattled her how deeply Parc dug through her past.

"So that recording," Layne said. Parc shot her a look. "Indulge me a second." She needed to speak before she lost courage. He smiled at her then, the type of smile that went with a pat on the head.

Layne moved the food around on her plate, pulling off the pizza crust and shredding it, unable to digest it. Then, the takeout boxes had to be rearranged and so did the condiments, and she took her time doing it all. Parc moved between answering texts and his early dinner, stopping at times to laugh at a video he must have been watching on Facebook. If the revelation about his childhood brought back bad memories, it did not show. She cleared her throat.

"And those photos, the video?"

Parc didn't acknowledge her for a full minute. He turned up the volume a notch on whatever video he was playing on his social media. "I only caught them on audio, I'm afraid. Were you hoping for more?"

"With Marco. You took advantage of his exhaustion from all those jobs, his non-citizenship status."

Layne forced herself to remain calm. She was not her mother or her brother. No more throwing things. She could have fun. She did what her therapist taught her to do and imagined listening to quiet blue waves kissing the coastline, the sand bleached white. Nothing but nature for miles, until she heard the roar of the waves and she was in control of her mind again.

"I asked you something," she said finally.

"You have a lot on your mind today. So many questions, it's hard to follow."

"Try," Layne said. She had outmatched Parc today. Parc sighed and stretched his arms over his head. She could wait.

"Okay. Here goes. Marco did you a favor. You should mail him a gift. Look where you are now, where we both are. Leagues above our other positions. I'm using the dessert as bait. First, we finish the schedule."

Layne ran her tongue along her teeth and blew her nose. She got up and filled her water bottle, taking her time at the water cooler. Then, she sipped slowly, tapping her foot on the floor.

"You're right, I get the signal. Where are my manners?" Parc put his phone away. "Sorry, I'm with you again. You were saying something about the website or was it the schedule?"

"Oh, the schedule," she said. Her voice was tense. "It's one step forward, two steps back." Layne saw the half-eaten food from one restaurant; the side dishes from another; the hot maple syrup drinks he had picked up at a third place; the bottled water.

When he arrived, Parc unfolded a red and white checkered tablecloth from his briefcase, it smelled like laundry detergent and dryer sheets. He smoothed it over the only other desk that she had been using as a table for her meals for the last two weeks. It was down the hall from her desk, so it gave her the illusion of getting away from her work while she ate, even when she brought both her phone and laptop with her. There was a cardboard cake box with a pink ribbon tied around it with promised fudge brownies topped with salted caramel ice cream inside. The box was in a portable cooler bag to keep the ice cream from melting. She could smell the sugary aroma.

The compliments, the childhood confessions, the locked doors. Titillation came to mind. The forced intimacy. Two years of it. Parc rested so comfortably in the office chair; it had taken on his shape. Anyone who stepped in would say this was extravagant, the intention was unmistakable.

Layne followed Parc's eyes roaming her body when he spoke to her, he could not keep his hands away. Always reaching for something in her space, bumping into wherever she happened to be with his hips, his shoulders, his ankles. Yes, she loved the attention dammit. Part of her did. The admission was on the table. He made her feel more important than her parents ever had, more than even Rael could from so far away.

The taboo was broken. Layne, who grew up invisible, enjoyed being noticed, needed to be noticed. This want was buried so deep inside of her, she pretended it did not exist, but the intensity of it would not die down. It came to her how little attention Marvyn received from her parents growing up and how much West was willing to give. Plates and plates full of attention, all for Marvyn. Enough to die for.

Chapter 44

A buzz. Layne picked up her phone.

A smirk tugged at the corners of her lips as she imagined the hefty fine Rael would have to cough up and the red flag that would mark his name the next time he attempted to enter the country.

There was more brightness for Layne. Virginia and James were not a thing anymore. It was okay for him to have a wife but not okay for his girlfriend to stray. He confirmed this on a park bench halfway between Hamilton and Toronto, where she had asked him to meet. Layne flipped to her photo gallery and deleted the recording of Virginia and Rael. She was done with that, too. There was nothing left to wait for. She pressed forward on an email in her inbox and then one more. Motion took over. She grabbed the largest empty takeout bag, marched down the hall to her desk, opened her briefcase, and threw in what was hers: papers; stapler coffee mug; pen; diary.

High-heeled boots clicked rapidly on the tiles. She filled the bag: headphones; charging station; laptop stand; portable heater; screen cleaner. She would leave the ferns and the curtains for the new students.

"Hey," Parc said. His voice was sharp. He cleared his throat. "I need your help with the best dessert in the province. There's something in it guaranteed to make you thirsty after and I know a place where they take care of that."

He positioned himself on her desk, so that his knees brushed her hands that were still emptying her drawer. She could feel the cold of the steel drawer on her hand. "We could skip back to Toronto, have a night out. You could crash on my couch, or anywhere you want."

"Goodbye, Parc. I'm sure you'll find another job. You can always head back to the U.K. Tell Rinata not to overwater the plants."

"What?"

"I'm such a dummy. There's no way around this. Virginia was right. You took advantage of your boss's leave to get me down here. Alone, lonely, isolated."

"You're listening to that slut now?"

"You don't deny it?"

"People who don't have your best interests at heart get all of your attention and you ignore those who really care for you. It's your Achilles' heel."

"And another thing, I owe you a recording. Check your messages." Parc reached for his phone. There was a game of Monopoly on his desk. Layne had not noticed it before. He leaned on his desk and the game tumbled out, pieces flew everywhere, and she crushed a few under her heels.

"Oh, your game. It seems to be ruined," Layne said. "Watch where you step."

"Is this your idea of a joke?" he mumbled. Ignoring the mess at his feet, he pressed play in his WhatsApp.

"My name is Marco Monopolis, a Canadian citizen. I accepted inflated grades from Mr. Parc Watterson. We all did. In exchange, I helped fire Miss Layne Fortunefield, so that he could hire her back. Let me explain."

Parc was playing the rest of the recording Marco sent her, the same one he forwarded to James. Then, the bang of the door blotted everything out.

Chapter 45

In two weeks, Layne would be homeless. She had two more Fridays in this apartment. Fourteen days and fourteen nights. Or was it fourteen days and thirteen nights and one more Friday, but two more of all of the other weekdays? Layne's mind got busy with calculations. She saw everything through the lens of moving now, something her childhood had prepared her for. Though nothing had changed, in her mind she was occupied: relocating items she had so recently unpacked except, like her, they had nowhere to go. There was no longer any point in replacing the ketchup or refilling the salt shaker. She cancelled the repair person for the leaky sink and the ripped screen door. Dust piled up on the bookshelves and she kept her hands away from the furniture polish and rags.

By April 1, this place would be Rinata's new home and Layne would be living out of boxes, desperate to reground herself somewhere. The thought of another new neighborhood so soon with its unfamiliar noises and strange scenery made her feel as though the world was ending.

Only the memory of the look on Parc's face as she banged the door behind her cheered her up. Layne pressed delete again. She would not stay on as a teacher for James, a man who never sent a text or answered his phone when she was the one trying to reach him. James was too tied to Virginia, even if he had stopped seeing her, had fired Parc, and used his connections to get Rael stopped at the airport. They were even now.

Rinata was already welcomed as the new branch director, a position that was always hers. Layne faced the choice of either staying in Hamilton, finding a place to live, and seeking a new way to support herself, or moving back to Toronto and doing the same there.

She was dressed in shorts and a t-shirt. Instead of lying on her mat and stretching away her anxieties, she Googled Ottawa real estate news, as if she expected the sale of her grandmother's house to be on the front page. There would be an accompanying photo of her parents wiring her half the money next to a beaming Mr. Star.

Even in this imaginary, absurd photo, she saw Marvyn lurking in the background as he had been that night, covered in blood. Determined to terrify her. Then, the image of his body in the car and the sound of him moaning. The waiter at the café with huge sweat rings under his armpits and close-set eyes was West. She was sure of it. He had followed them the whole time, somehow managed to get to Marvyn, overpower him, and take the car.

"Stop, Layne. For the love of heaven, stop." She was speaking to no one in full knowledge that she needed brakes for her brain. There was only one place she could think of to get them. A day was circled in her calendar with the note: end of vacation. He had to be back by now. Something clicked in her mind as she dug in the kitchen drawer for her car keys. Could she handle rejection? She had never appeared without an appointment before. She would not be turned away.

The lightbulbs stared; each electrical outlet was larger than it should have been. She checked that all the lights were off and that nothing was plugged in, going back three times to make sure the door was locked before punching his office address into Google Maps.

In Toronto, Layne begged for a session from outside his locked office door, followed him into the crowded elevator, and out to the airless underground parking lot. Her heels clacked on the concrete; her untethered wild hair trapped in the strap of her purse.

"You're still processing," the therapist said after they had looked at each other for a few extra minutes. "How long did you say the drive was?

Layne felt the moment he relented like the loosening of a cramp in her stomach. She didn't say a word as he abandoned his plans for going home, reopened the office, shivered while the heat returned, and blinked as the lights came back on.

The office was refurnished, so altered Layne didn't recognize it. She was thrown by the couch that was too grey and too velvet; she could not decide if it was bigger or smaller than the previous one. Her familiar spot was gone, and now she had to make a new one, adding to her discomfort and her sense of being in the wrong place at the right time.

"This was a regression. Full-blown. I've taken so many steps back, I can't even count them. It started with one—an absurd text message I should have deleted immediately before my next breath."

"As you said in the parking lot."

Layne accepted the dig, she deserved it. It was not that she was trying to be repetitive, she could not settle. Even the carpet was different, a muted mustard that made her want to vomit. She paced, wrung her hands, smoothed her hair into a ponytail over and over again, but had no elastic to hold it, so it ended up scattered down her back.

"Slow down. By regression, do you mean a retreat?"

He took a long sip of ginger tea, and Layne made a face at the gurgling sound in his throat as he swallowed. Everything was off today. She had to stay focused. This was an emergency appointment. He had been away for so long and had gotten backed up. Of course, she understood.

"Retreat as in withdrawal?" she asked, jumping as a police car whizzed by outside, sirens blaring.

"No, as in self-deception." He warmed his hands on the mug; Layne's fingers were ice cold. She imagined his heated hands covering her eyes and flipping open: peekaboo.

The mug hit the glass table too hard and teetered on the edge. He inched it back along with his chair when Layne wanted him closer.

"Layne? You're not ready. We cannot go overtime tonight. You can reschedule."

"No, no, no." Layne covered her own eyes with her cold hands and mouthed the word "yes" and then "Rael."

"I'm sorry. Could you speak up?"

"Yes," she said. Clearing her throat, her mouth as dry as stone, she stretched out her arm, drained his mug for him without taking her eyes off his, and wiped her mouth with the napkin stuck to the bottom of it. The mug had absorbed enough heat that she could still be warmed by it.

"Yes. Rael," she yelled, clinging to the mug.

"You can speak normally. I understand you deceived yourself about Rael? That's not a small thing. Would you like your own tea? I offered."

Layne's smile was full of gratitude, her hands covered her eyes once again. He would wait for her to drink her tea first. Layne could smell the added avocado-flavored honey, and listened while he drank, while he shifted in his seat.

When Layne was able to drop her hands from her face, she met the therapist's eyes. They were the kindest she had seen in so long that she wanted them to stay on her, to hold her down like nails so she could not screw up again. His gaze on her was what held her together, something she was afraid to admit. He knew her secrets: that denial had helped her survive at times, more times than she wanted to count. Sometimes admitting a truth forced her to relive it, which was worse than living it the first time.

"It was Marvyn who tried to get you to sign away something he didn't own anymore, and not in the most palatable manner. Did the lawyer lie to you about West's death? Was West working downstairs the whole time in the café, conspiring with your parents as Marvyn suggested? Was West's fiancée in on it? Or was she counterfeit, too? There's an awful lot of deception swirling around. Are you sure about Rael? I thought you had come to terms with the fact that he did not betray you, not strictly. You threw him out. Technically, broke up with him. I would like to understand."

Layne would make him understand at her own pace. She said to the therapist, "Keep your eyes on me. I'll split in two. Don't you dare look away."

"Oh, Layne," he said. "I'm right here."

"I went by a popcorn shop," she said.

"Popcorn?"

"Yes, gourmet and this is what happened."

* * *

There was a gourmet popcorn shop somewhere between Toronto's China Town and Little Italy. The place smelled savory and sweet from outside, and Layne could not resist entering. It was impossible to ignore the light atmosphere, and she wanted to let it in. After ridding herself of Parc and her job in one shot, she needed to balance herself out, achieve mental homeostasis. Entering in a favorite long coat that was already too warm for the March weather, Layne looked around for a place to hang it.

"Try this." A familiar voice, like sweet hot chutney. "It'll be cold just now."

"Mmm. Rocky Road. The power of sugar. You chose it on purpose."

"So, what if I did?"

Few women spoke English in a Quebecois accent in Toronto. Of course, there were tourists. Out of the corner of her eye, Layne glimpsed a slim blonde with a blunt haircut, wearing a leather skirt with lace trim. There was no need to see more, not if she knew what was good for her. But she could not help it. Logical thoughts leaped off the tracks of her brain. As she turned her head another inch and then another, her feet facing the opposite direction, Layne felt pain shoot from her jawline down to her shoulder blade due to the deep twist.

"Now try this," Rael said. He placed a toasted kernel on Virginia's tongue. Her mouth was already open. Cinnamon roll, Pina colada, parmesan. Pop, pop, pop. Layne could taste all of it in her nostrils, at the back of her mouth, under her tongue—a blend that together activated her gag reflex.

Fast, fast, fast. She had to move. Layne tried running all the way back to Hamilton, seeing nothing in front of her but a whirl of color, yet the taste of sickeningly sweet popcorn persisted in her mouth.

At some point, she had such a sharp cramp in her side that it was all she could do to flag an Uber. Unable to work her phone, she crawled into the back, paying the driver extra to take her around until her mind could stay in her body.

It was only when she arrived back at her apartment that she realized she had forgotten her coat. The realization hit her like another loss, another thing she loved slipping away from her. She could not shake the absurdity of choosing such a warm coat on a hot day and then foolishly taking it off in the first place.

Chapter 46

The doorbell rang while Layne was in the shower. She stopped mid-rinse and stuck her head out from behind the curtain, squinting to see the time on her phone through the steam. Shivering, she dried her hand on a towel, and held her phone outside of the water. Almost midnight.

The bell rang again, long and shrill. Layne turned off first one tap and then the other, and wrapped herself in a towel. The ringing turned into knocking, then banging. She wrapped another towel around her dripping hair, stuck her wet feet into her slippers, and padded into the living room to the front door. She looked through the peephole, unlocked the door, and opened it a crack.

On the other side of the door was Rael, neck bent against the wind, stamping his feet in the cold. One hand was deep in his coat pocket, and the other held a bouquet of long-stemmed red roses. He must have talked his way around the customs officials, not the ending she imagined for him. An intensity of emotion almost knocked Layne over. Rael's breath was visible in the air, and he had a winter cap pulled low over his ears. He no longer looked like a tourist.

Everything about him made Layne feel so alert. Not an hour passed when she didn't think of him, and she felt the dull ache in her chest that was the space he used to fill. She longed to have her boyfriend back, except he no longer existed, if he ever did. This truth clamped down on her, and the thoughts that life without Rael was the wrong vanished.

"Showering so late?" Rael said. Before Layne could answer, he continued, "You were hoping I had been deported."

"I can shower whenever I want and you said that line on the phone. I'm not having the same conversation twice."

"Your little payback cost me a packet," Rael said.

"You said that, too."

"But I am not a grudge holder. We're still friends, right? Can we agree on that?"

"There's nothing for us to agree on," Layne said. His eyes held her attention. "You said you had some things of mine to return at some point, and your things are over there." Layne nodded to a box on the table, already sealed with moving tape.

Layne had packed all of Rael's belongings: sweaters, books, hoodies, lotions. She didn't want them anymore and it was part of her agenda for tomorrow—returning his items with all of their accompanying emotions. There was a puddle of water at her feet. Her eyes met his again, and she burned with a mixture of desire and pain. She longed to throw her arms around him and felt a stab, remembering.

"What happened to 'coming by in the morning'?" Layne repeated when he didn't answer. She let him in, locking the door behind him. It took some time to relock; the door was breaking along with so many things in the apartment. Goosebumps appeared on her arms and legs, and Rael did not hide his stare. Let him.

"For you," he said. Layne took the flowers in one hand and placed them on the dining room table. She would decide what to do with them when he left. Her thank-you banged up against her front teeth.

"I thought we'd talk now. You sounded like..." He shrugged.

"Sounded like what?" Layne asked.

"I got this feeling after you called about your move tomorrow," Rael answered. "You must be freezing."

He took off his jacket to drape around her, and Layne jumped out of reach. He stared at her in such a way that she felt how much she loved him, and how painful their separation would be for some time to come.

"I have to dress. Excuse me."

In her bedroom, Layne put on a pair of jeans and a sweater, her legs and arms still damp sticking to her body. She jammed her feet back into her slippers, blow-dried her hair, and applied anti-itch cream all over her neck. She counted the boxes in her room a dozen times, first by twos, then by threes and fives.

When Layne came out of her bedroom, she hoped Rael would be gone, but he had sunk into her couch with his head in his hands, rubbing his temples. He hadn't bothered to turn on a light in the living room, so the only light came from the dining room where she had placed the flowers that were so long, they touched both ends of the table.

"Ready to step out?" he said.

"It's a little late," Layne said.

"How does it make you feel? That I'm here." It was only then that Layne noticed the black jewelry box in his hand. Layne's thoughts were her own, and she had no desire to count, or to leave her body, or to step out.

"This isn't going to work," she said, shaking her head. "It's not how I want it. It just is."

"What do you mean? We've both had our time to think. You don't really believe that woman meant anything?"

"Virginia isn't my roommate anymore, and you're not my boyfriend anymore. Please leave."

"Are there no bumps in the road in your new world? We can get over this. You've been a kind of a hero in a way, how you dealt with everything, moved on your own for the first time in your life. I guess you were finally ready to fly."

"Come on, Rael, we both need to get some sleep. I have an interview in the morning at the University of Toronto. I want to finish my MA. Parc was right about that, and about you, as it turns out. It is not okay that you came over when we made a plan for tomorrow. You're trying to catch me off guard."

"Prophet Parc, yeah? Or is it Playboy Parc?" Rael asked. When Layne didn't answer, he continued, "What do you take me for? I missed you, I've missed you every day, every minute. No, I couldn't wait until the morning. It's called love."

"Love, eh? I saw you at the popcorn place putting love into Virginia's mouth, not for the first time."

Neither of them said anything for a minute. Layne noticed Rael slipped the jewelry box back into his coat pocket; he would be sure not to leave it behind if things didn't go his way. He was always so organized.

"You have everything all wrong," Rael said. "This last little while has messed with your head. It would mess with anyone's. Nobody meant for any of this to happen."

"Nobody meant for me to find out, you mean."

"You've given me a hard time, if you haven't noticed. You threw me out after I'd driven five hours to be with you, only slightly after I'd flown across the world to be with you. You have a part to play, and you got your revenge. I tried to leave and got into a mess at the airport, so I changed my mind and stayed. You didn't think of that, I bet? You thought it would be so easy to get rid of me. Sit next to me instead of circling around me, and let's speak properly."

"This is as proper as it's going to get, Rael."

"I might feel guilty, but I don't feel responsible, you know."

"As if there's a difference," Layne said, crossing her arms over her chest. She wiped her mouth with the back of her hand and tasted the bitter bottom-of-the-soap from the empty bottle in the shower. "Parc had your number from the beginning. He knew exactly what was wrong with you."

"Hmm. Is there an echo in here? Parc this and Parc that. What were you getting up to with him in Hamilton? Getting even or a consolation prize?"

Layne swallowed hard and wished her voice wasn't so thick. She didn't want to cry; it wouldn't change anything.

"Get out."

In the dim light, it was hard to tell if Rael had turned color with emotion, or was sitting in too much shadow.

"Stop pretending. You don't really want me to go. You'll be phoning me tomorrow, begging me to take a step back."

Layne raced to the dining room table in four giant steps, snatched the bouquet of long-stemmed roses, raised them up high, and smashed Rael over the head with them. Red velvet petals exploded all over Rael, the couch, the floor.

"Liar!" she yelled. Smash, smash. "Liar! How could you do this to me?"

"Layne, darling, please. Please." He tried to block his face with his arms.

"You laughed at me," she said. "You could not choose a stranger from the party, any stranger, no, you had to choose her. You both laughed at me."

Layne hit and hit and hit Rael with the flowers until there was nothing left but stems and a carpet of leaves and flower heads.

Chapter 47

Layne changed her mind about her coat the next day. It was a flattering coat that made her look taller; she had bought it her first winter in the city, and there was no reason to give it up. It made sense at the time to leave it there, but she didn't have to give any more of herself away.

The gourmet popcorn place might have kept it for her. The University of Toronto MA advisor had sent her a text that he could not meet until this afternoon, and the last thing she wanted to do was hang around a packed-up, blank-walled apartment. Layne could not bear to look at the mess of flowers on her living room floor or at the box with Rael's name on it in her own handwriting. She would slip the movers extra to clean up and deliver the box to Virginia. Outside of the eatery, she paused, took a deep breath, and pushed the memory of Rael feeding Virginia popcorn as far into the back of her mind as she could.

"Hey, Miss Fortunefield."

Layne turned around, and it was Marco wearing a "trust-me-I'm-tour-guide" t-shirt.

"You're giving those gourmet food walking tours?" Layne asked. "I wish I had such a flexible skillset."

"I quit yesterday. The hospital called me. I'm starting my old job as a nurse next week. Got to get my puppy toilet-trained in time."

"That's great. Congratulations." She remembered how much she had always liked Marco, how she had taken it for granted that once the English course was over they would be real friends, and how the idea had absorbed some of her loneliness.

"What are you doing here?" Marco asked.

"Thought I'd grab a snack, treat myself."

"I could give you a free tour. One-on-one. You'll be so impressed with my English."

Layne had no desire for a tour; she didn't want to know the history of this place. Her own story was enough. The truth, Layne.

"Actually, I forgot my coat here the other day."

"Oh." His face fell. "Why didn't you call first? Ask them to hold it before someone takes it."

"How do you know I didn't?"

"The look on your face," Marco said. "We could still do the tour."

"Maybe another time," Layne answered. "And by the way, I've always been impressed with your English. What are you doing here?"

"Picking up my last paycheck. I want to take a few days off before I start overnight shift work again."

There was a pause between them.

"Don't you still want your coat?"

"Not really."

"I don't understand."

"I feel blocked about going in there right this minute."

In her mind, Layne saw Rael with his finger in Virginia's mouth. The two of them laughing. She fought a wave of dizziness. She stepped out of the way of a couple, each walking two Labradors on four leashes. She longed to pet them, and bury her face in soft fur.

Layne fiddled with her car keys, tracing her fingers over the edges, into each groove. Why were they so slippery? The oil she kept to lower her anxiety must have opened in her purse. She could feel it seeping into every item, as though she were inside of her purse, too. She would have to go in somewhere, rinse it out in a bathroom, but not here.

"I get you," Marco said, snapping her back to attention. "You must listen to your body's signals, interpret your own mind. Sometimes I take a different route home every day for a week to change my luck. Works every time." Marco took off his glasses, wiped them clean with a cloth from his pocket. "Why don't you let me get it?"

"Would you?" A weight lifted off Layne. "Here's a photo." She took her phone out of her back pocket and scrolled through it, noticing the look of recognition on Marco's face when she showed him a shot of her in the coat. She was grateful when he didn't tell her where he had seen that coat before. Without thinking, she shoved the phone into her purse. Marco held up one finger, and Layne tried not to look at her purse, so she wouldn't drag his attention to the oily stain that must be expanding on the bottom.

"Hey, Miss Fortunefield." Marco sauntered out of the eatery a few minutes later, bringing a wave of sweet popcorn smell with him. "Victory." He held up her coat like an offering. "You are lucky. This is a very good sign for whatever else you planned for today. Luck comes in columns."

"Columns? In English, people say waves."

"You can stop teaching me English."

"You can stop calling me Miss Fortunefield. It's Layne."

"All right. Can I help carry the coat for you, Layne?"

Layne met Marco's eyes. They were bright, as bright as his smile and the dimple in his right cheek. The truth was, she had loved tutoring him all those afternoons. He was a great student, and he made her laugh.

"Have you eaten today?" Marco asked. "I got my paycheck." He patted his pocket.

"Who still gets paychecks?"

"You're right. Tips. That's the word. Are you hungry or not? Come on, everybody is hungry all of the time, right? For something, anyway, and sometimes food is all there is." Their eyes met again. Layne was happy she was not the type to blush, or she would now.

"I do owe you a meal," Layne said.

"You don't really, but I don't want to eat alone if I don't have to. Empty plates invite bad luck. You digest better when you're with someone." Marco held out his arm, and Layne took it. Marco wasn't as tall as Rael, so it was much less of an effort to stroll beside him.

Layne's iPhone rang in her purse, and a familiar uneasiness took over her. If she answered it, she would have oily hands until she could get to a bathroom to wash them; she wouldn't be able to touch anything until then, and the cold faucet would slip and slide when she did find one.

The university advisor wouldn't change their meeting time again; it had to be someone else. Her body tingled with the knowledge that she wasn't ready for whatever or whoever it was on the other end.

Dopamine hits come and go; Layne didn't have to answer, didn't have to let anyone into her universe if she didn't want them there. The ringing stopped. Then, nothing for a step, and then the beep of a text.

"I like someone who can ignore the phone," Marco said, not bothering to raise his voice over the traffic, so Layne had to lean in closer to him. "I remember you taught us about iPhone separation. A good lesson, not as good as the one Mr. Parc taught us."

"Which one was that?"

"Think about it. He mocked both of us, and mockers should never be ignored. We ignored this bad behavior because we were afraid of him. Still, I'll remember for next time. You should, too. I'm sorry for my part in hurting you."

Layne's phone beeped again, plus two more after that, but this was a guess, an estimate. Layne wasn't counting. Right now, she was hungry and looking forward to lunch with Marco and then, her interview at the university.

She imagined her grandmother looking down on her now, waving the inheritance money and could not resist. She pulled out the phone. It wasn't as slippery as she had thought it would be. Ten seconds, no more. No. She put it back. She would not give in to a phone. Missing every detail did not scare her anymore. Her grandmother would be insulted if she answered now after everything she had learned.

"We were afraid of him, weren't we?"

"You don't agree?"

"I do. Fear is a big deal. Did you know scientists have transmitted fear in mice two generations?" she said. All she could see of the city was glass, chrome, and pavement. She refused to let it blind her. "They chose a certain smell and scared them to death with it. Their children and grandchildren retained the fear of the smell."

"How do you scare someone with a smell?" Marco asked. Layne watched as he noticed his own reflection passing by another shiny building and didn't bother to stop. This is something Rael would never have done. She kept on going too.

"Like they smell something and get an electric shock?" Marco continued in his accent that no longer sounded heavy. "Traumatize them by making them watch a mouse friend die? Or they pretend they killed it?"

"Good questions," Layne said in her teacher voice, then cleared her throat. Important information about her financial inheritance was out there waiting for her somewhere, and here she was thinking about her other inheritance; her emotional legacy. "Isn't that something?" she said. "What we inherit?"

Acknowledgements

Creating a novel is truly a collaborative effort, and I am immensely grateful to all those who have supported me along the way. Heartfelt thanks to my original writing partners, Rivka Begun and Babette Dunkelgrün, whose weekly Zoom sessions provided invaluable encouragement and motivation throughout the first draft—an achievement in itself.

I am deeply appreciative of Marc Kornblatt for his early feedback and unwavering enthusiasm, as well as SCBWI-Israel for facilitating our first meeting. My journey in English-language writing in Israel began with the Shaindy Rudoff MA in Creative Writing Program at Bar Ilan University, and I am forever indebted to them for opening the door to this path. May Shaindy's memory be a blessing.

A special appreciation goes to my publisher, AOS, and Michael Occhionero for their professionalism and patience.

I am also endlessly grateful for the unwavering support of my husband, Darron, who stands by my side through every novel, and to our children—Aryeh, Sivana, Gabriella, Meira, and Keren Ohr—for their love and understanding.

Excerpt from the poem "The Remains" granted from the author Susie Berg.